O HAPPY DAY

AND OTHER
TINYBURG TALES
It's never too late to go back and visit.

Robert J. Hastings

BROADMAN PRESS
NASHVILLE, TENNESSEE

© Copyright 1992 • Broadman Press
All Rights Reserved

4257-41

ISBN: 0-8054-5741-0
Dewey Decimal Classification: SC
Subject Heading: SHORT STORIES // CHRISTIAN LIFE—FICTION
Library of Congress Catalog Card Number: 92-10193

Printed in the United States of America

All Scripture quotations are from the King James Version
of the Bible.

Library of Congress Cataloging-in-Publication Data

Hastings, Robert J.
  O happy day and other Tinyburg tales / Robert J. Hastings.
     p.   cm.
  ISBN 0-8054-5741-0
  1. Christian fiction, American.   I. Title.
PS3558.A727015   1992
813'.54—dc20   92-10193
                                                                  CIP

O HAPPY DAY AND
OTHER TINYBURG TALES

Dedicated to
Craig Robert Jessup
Laurel E. Hastings
Anne E. Hastings

Other Books by Robert J. Hastings

Tinyburg Tales
Tinyburg Revisited
The Answer Book for Writers and Storytellers
A Nickel's Worth of Skim Milk
A Penny's Worth of Minced Ham

Foreword

This is my third collection of fiction about the mythical village of Tinyburg, "The only city in the United States with an unlisted zip code."

Previous titles were *Tinyburg Tales* and *Tinyburg Revisited.*

These are stories I've enjoyed telling on my weekly radio program, "Tinyburg Tales," as well as to a wide spectrum of church, school, civic, and senior-adult audiences.

In this edition I'm also including, in the front matter, the full text of my popular essay, "The Station." This essay, referred to in the opening story, has been widely reprinted in the syndicated columns of Ann Landers, *Reader's Digest*, and various anthologies.

Although I did not have children in mind when I began writing short stories, I have been pleasantly surprised to learn how many boys and girls enjoy reading or hearing them. Fortunate are those children whose parents find time to read to them, go with them to libraries, and encourage them to listen to wholesome radio which, far more than television, fosters imagination and creativity in younger minds.

—Robert J. Hastings

O Happy Day is fiction, and any resemblance to actual persons, living or dead, is coincidental.

"The Station"

Tucked away in our subconscious minds is an idyllic vision in which we see ourselves on a long journey that spans an entire continent. We're traveling by train and, from the windows, we drink in the passing scenes of cars on nearby highways, of children waving at crossings, of cattle grazing in distant pastures, of smoke pouring from power plants, of row upon row of cotton and corn and wheat, of flatlands and valleys, of city skylines and village halls.

But uppermost in our minds is our final destination—for at a certain hour and on a given day, our train will finally pull into the station with bells ringing, flags waving, and bands playing. And once that day comes, so many wonderful dreams will come true. So restlessly, we pace the aisles and count the miles, peering ahead, waiting, waiting, waiting for the station.

"Yes, when we reach the station, that will be it!" we promise ourselves. "When we're eighteen...win that promotion...put the last kid through college... buy that 450 SL Mercedes Benz...pay off the mortgage...have a nest egg for retirement."

From that day on we will all live happily ever after.

Sooner or later, however, we must realize there is no station in this life, no one earthly place to arrive at once and for all. The journey is the joy. The station is an illusion—it constantly outdistances us. Yesterday's a memory, tomorrow's a dream. Yesterday belongs to a history, tomorrow belongs to God. Yesterday's a fading sunset, tomorrow's a faint sunrise. Only today is there light enough to love and live.

So gently close the door on yesterday and throw the key away. It isn't the burdens of today that drive men mad, but rather the regret over yesterday and the fear of tomorrow.

"Relish the moment" is a good motto, especially when coupled with Psalm 118:24, "This is the day which the Lord hath made; we will rejoice and be glad in it."

So stop pacing the aisles and counting the miles. Instead, swim more rivers, climb more mountains, kiss more babies, count more stars. Laugh more and cry less. Go barefoot oftener. Eat more ice cream. Ride more merry-go-rounds. Watch more sunsets. Life must be lived as we go along.

—Bob

Contents

O Happy Day

Although February 3 dawned gray and cold in Tinyburg, it told of sunshine and good times for the Spiller family. A color-splashed flyer from Willow Creek State Park announced the good news.

"Look!" cried Ted, ripping open the envelope. "A big lodge overlooking the lake, swimming beach, campsites and trailer hookups, fishing, boating, a playground with slides and swings, nature trails, horseback riding, shuffleboard, even a golf course.

"Why chase up and down the interstates spending a fortune, when we can enjoy a fun vacation only three hours from home?"

"Daddy," asked eight-year-old Rhonda, "would we be happy on a camping vacation?"

13

"Happy? Did you say happy? You'll be so happy you won't know your name's Rhonda Spiller."

It being their first time to camp, the Spillers began laying in supplies long before school was out: a new tent, sleeping bags, ground tarp, rain fly, Coleman lantern, propane stove, grill and charcoal, new swimming outfits and rugged camp clothes, an iron skillet, plastic water bucket, paper cups and plates, mosquito netting, extra flashlights, garbage bags, an ice chest, and a first aid kit.

All told, I believe their checklist totaled 181 items. You're probably not interested in a breakdown, but it also included lawn chairs, insect repellant, suntan lotion, broad-brimmed hats and sunglasses, a camera and eight rolls of film, storybooks, a hatchet, a hammock, small microwave oven, extra extension cords, towels and blankets, fishing rods, golf clubs, clothes line rope, and a transistor radio.

Plus the food: lots of canned fruits and meats, cooking oil, baby food, soft drinks, can opener, chips and snacks, and every instant food on the market: instant oatmeal, coffee, Kool Aid, lemonade, potatoes, soup, pancake mix, hot chocolate, and puddings.

Oh, yes. At the last minute they bought a

new camcorder to make videos and decided to take the baby's stroller and playpen.

By August, their breezeway looked like a Walmart! Candice advised Ted to practice putting up the tent in the back yard. "Practice?" he said, as if she'd suggested he practice how to brush his teeth. "I was an Eagle Scout; I can put up a tent blindfolded."

Two weeks before camp, Rhonda, the family worrywart, again wondered if they'd be happy.

Ted guaranteed she would, even typing a schedule for her as well as Ruthie, age ten, and Randy, age eleven months:

Rhonda's Happy List

Swimming	Horseback riding
Sunbathing	Meeting new friends
Sandcastles	TV in the lodge
Puzzles	Video games in the lodge
Crafts	Collecting butterflies
Monopoly	Reading
Kickball	Listening to tapes
Making photos	Cookouts
Nature hikes	Teasing Ruthie

On Sunday afternoon the grandparents, Clay and Edith Barker, offered to help them load up for an early start on Monday. This was probably a mistake. Since Randy was teething and running a slight fever, Grandma insisted he stay home with her instead of being "turned loose in the woods."

"But Mother," argued Candice, "Willow Creek isn't the end of the world. They do have electricity, running water and telephones. This is a family outing—we'd miss Randy."

"And Randy would miss being happy," said Rhonda. "See, Daddy made him his own little happy list."

"Some things are more important than happiness," replied Grandma, "such as common sense. I won't rest a minute while you're gone."

Grandpa supervised the loading. After three hours of tugging and sweating, the van was ready, the playpen and stroller tied on top. There was barely room for Ted and Candice and the car seat in front, and for Rhonda to sit on Ruthie's lap in the back.

"Oh, the ice chest!" screamed Candice, dashing into the house. "It has our soft drinks and sandwiches for Monday's lunch."

Grandpa ordered everyone to stand back and he'd find room for the chest. "Have to put it on the bottom," he warned. "Otherwise it might tip over and spill water on everything."

"But what if we need a cold drink on the way?" wondered Candice.

"It's less than three hours," argued Ted. "Can't we last that long?"

Sensing the tension, Rhonda asked her daddy if they had to wait until tomorrow to start being happy.

"Rhonda, I wish you'd stop asking that question. You have your happy list. Now quit worrying."

Monday morning the Spillers were backing out of the drive when Grandpa showed up with a peck of peaches, a sack of apples, and a watermelon: "You need something fresh—junk food's not good for the kids."

"But Daddy, there's not room," protested Candice.

"Then I'll just dump the apples and peaches loose in the van, let them roll down and fill the cracks. And Candice, you hold the watermelon on your lap."

At last they were on their way. Grandpa waved vigorously, pleased he thought of the fruit.

Instead of taking the interstate, Ted decided on a shortcut. Candice reminded him it was a back road, seldom used, with stretches of gravel.

"This is a vacation, not the Indy 500," Ted

replied. "Pretty scenery along here. Relax and enjoy yourself."

The first hour, they met only two other cars. Then about forty miles from nowhere, a water hose burst, spewing clouds of steam over the hood and windshield.

"The car's on fire!" screamed Rhonda. "Help, let me out!"

Ted braked and pulled over. Hissing steam smothered the van with billows of white clouds. It was a mess, with all the coolant lost.

Warning no one to touch the hot engine, Ted left on foot for a phone. He was gone a long, long time. With no air conditioning in the van, the children grew restless and fussy. Candice reached for some cold drinks, then remembered the ice chest was at the bottom of everything.

Maybe a slice of watermelon would taste good, but the knives were packed, too. In desperation, she split the melon on a sharp rock and let the girls eat it with their hands, the way squirrels hold nuts.

They were quite a mess when Ted and a serviceman came back in a pickup. "What happened? Did the watermelon slip out of your hands?"

When Candice said she dropped it on purpose, Ted scolded her for wasting so much of it. She replied that if he was so worried over a little watermelon, he could get down on his knees and eat the leftovers.

Ted refused the offer—bigger problems lay ahead. The new hose was too short! Another trip to town, more delays. A whole day of vacation ruined, Candice complained, just "to see the scenery on a lonely back road."

It was dusk and misting rain when they reached their camp site. "We're starved," cried the girls. "Me, too," answered Ted, "but it's more important to set up the tent so we can have a dry place to sleep."

Although Ted had boasted he was an Eagle Scout, for some reason all the pieces of the new tent wouldn't fit. While everyone held flashlights for him to read the instructions, he finally succeeded. By now the mist had turned to a slow drizzle. Little Randy, still running a slight fever, was flushed and restless. They snacked on Grandpa's apples and peaches, then hurried to bed. Before falling asleep, Rhonda begged, "Daddy, will we be happy tomorrow?"

Then, from the next tent, someone began playing a harmonica:

O happy day that fixed my choice
On thee, my Savior and my God!
Well may this glowing heart rejoice,

And tell its raptures all abroad.
Happy day, happy day,
When Jesus washed my sins away!

—*Philip Doddridge*

I'm glad *someone's* happy," said Candice.

When they got up Tuesday morning, it was still muggy, humid, overcast. Mosquitoes were like dive-bombers. Because their sleeping bags got wet in the night, Ted said they had to hang them up to dry before even thinking about breakfast. In desperation, Candice opened the ice chest and served the sandwiches and soft drinks intended for the day before. "I always wanted to drink a Dr. Pepper for breakfast," grinned Rhonda.

The girls hung around camp all morning, saying it was too hot and wet to do anything.

At noon, Ted listened to the farm and weather reports on their transistor radio:

"Good news! The hot and humid weather that's roasted us for two days will end soon. A big cold front's building up in Canada. Once it reaches us, look for sunny, dry days with blue skies. Perfect for vacations."

"Goody-good-good," laughed Rhonda. "Tomorrow, we can all be happy!"

When the Spillers zipped up their sleeping bags Tuesday night, it was still muggy and rainy. From the next tent, someone again played "O Happy Day."

"I never want to hear that sad old hymn as long as I live," Candice said. Ted told himself he wished he'd never heard of Willow Creek State Park.

Would you believe Wednesday was a carbon copy of Tuesday? More rain, more sizzling temperatures, more promises of a cold front? And at bedtime, Rhonda again asked, "Daddy, will we be happy tomorrow?" while strains of "O Happy Day" drifted from the next campsite.

Thursday's weather report shocked the Spillers: "Folks, in all my years of forecasting, I've never seen anything like this. That cold front has apparently turned around and gone back to Canada! Our new forecast calls for more hot, steamy weather with intermittent showers. Maybe some relief next week."

Ted flipped the off button as if he were slapping a rattlesnake. "OK, kids, that's it. No silver lining for the Spillers, no happy days here. Come morning, we're heading back to Tinyburg."

"And will we be happy in Tinyburg?" asked Rhonda.

"You bet we'll be happy, once we're in the comfort of our air-conditioned den, stretched out on pallets, watching videos and eating homemade ice cream sodas."

Candice interrupted, "Girls, now that we've decided to go home in the morning, don't mope around camp the rest of the day. Find something to amuse yourselves—talk to the kids in the next tent."

This was a timely idea, for Ricki, a boy about Rhonda's age, just then asked if they'd like to go with him and his sisters to the happy place.

"Where's that?" asked Rhonda. "Is it on the happy list?"

"It's a secret place," Ricki whispered, "and is it fun!"

So the Spiller sisters joined Ricki along a beautiful wooded path that at times followed the lake, and at other times crossed high bluffs. At last they reached Ricki's happy place—where Willow Creek flows into Willow Creek Lake. The mouth of the creek was broad and shady, sheltered by big, leafy branches from giant trees—something like a canopy of foliage, a green cathedral.

"Watch me!" shouted Ricki as he kicked off his shoes and made a running leap for a thick, wild grapevine. With a Tarzan yell, Ricki swung out over the creek and flopped down into the clear water. What fun! All afternoon they took turns playing Tarzan, swinging and splashing. They were so happy they almost forgot supper.

Back in camp, both sets of parents had gotten acquainted and pooled their food for a cookout. "And Daddy!" Rhonda exclaimed. "Ricki showed us the happy place!"

The evening went well. There was a mystique, a magic about this new family. With the exception of Ricki, who seemed tired, the kids continued to laugh and play, while the parents swapped fishing stories and recipes. After everyone else was in bed, the fathers continued to sit by the fire, watching the red embers turn to gray. Ted, curious about the easy-going spirit of these new friends, asked for their secret.

Ricki's dad fell silent, almost sad, as if someone had reminded him of bad news. Then, "It's this way, Ted. Ricki is terminally ill. His doctor says six months, maybe a year. So we offered to take him anywhere this summer, maybe Disneyland. He surprised us by saying he'd like to go camping, something we'd never done as a family."

Ted interrupted, "Neither had we. But Ricki—does he know?"

"Ricki knows he's not well, but you saw how hard he played today. We're careful what we say. Doctors don't always know. One thing his Mom and I agreed on—we'd have a good time at Willow Creek, regardless. Knowing Ricki might not be here next summer, we can't wait for sunny days to have fun.

"And had you wondered who plays the harmonica each night? It's Ricki. He just loves 'O Happy Day,' the hymn our choir sang last Easter when he was baptized."

Then he reached in his pocket and handed Ted a copy of a short essay, "The Station," which compares life to a long journey by train, in which everyone is restless until they reach their destination. He said his favorite part reminds us of what we can do today, rather than waiting for tomorrow:

> So, swim more rivers, climb more mountains, kiss more babies, count more stars. Go barefoot oftener, eat more ice cream, watch more sunsets, ride more merry-go-rounds. Life must be lived as we go along.

Ted didn't know what to say. Both men were silent, listening to crickets in the distance.

The next morning, Friday, Ted announced he'd changed his mind: "We're staying until Saturday, as planned." They wouldn't leave early, rain or no rain. A new tone in his voice said today would be special. And it was! Both families packed picnic lunches and hiked to Ricki's secret place where all day, adults and kids, they splashed and played Tarzan on the wild grapevine.

When the Spillers broke camp on Saturday, they exchanged addresses with Ricki's parents, promising to keep in touch.

In the Tinyburg Church on Sunday morning, the Preacher chose for his text, "This is the day which the Lord hath made. We will rejoice and be glad in it" (Ps. 118:24). He quoted Blaise Pascal who said few of us live in the present. We use the present only to dream of the future. His exact words:

> So we never live, but we hope to live—and as we are always preparing to be happy, it is inevitable we should never be.

Ted bowed his head and thanked God for the wet, soggy vacation. He thanked God for Ricki's family who had shown—in a way he'd never known—that happiness is spelled T-O-D-A-Y.

On the way out, Ted bragged on the Preacher's message, but noted he heard a better one on his vacation.

"How's that? What church did you visit?"

When Ted told him about Ricki, the Preacher said he hoped his sermon was half as good as the one demonstrated on the wild grapevine.

School opened a couple of weeks later, and the leaves turned gold and crimson. The Spiller kids went trick-or-treatin' on Halloween and enjoyed Thanksgiving with their grandparents. In December, the Christmas lights emerged from their eleven-month slumber in packing boxes, and play practice began at the Tinyburg Church.

Shortly before New Year's, the Spillers received a belated Christmas card from Ricki's family. Inside, his dad had penciled this note:

This was Ricki's first Christmas in heaven. One of the last things he told me was, "Thanks, Dad, for taking me camping. It was fun. And I was happy!"

The Grapevine Swing

When I was a boy on the old plantation,
　Down by the deep bayou,
The fairest spot of all creation,
　Under the arching blue;
When the wind came over the cotton and corn,
　To the long slim loop I'd spring
With brown feet bare, and a hat-brim torn,
　And swing in the grapevine swing.

Swinging in the grapevine swing,
Laughing where the wild birds sing,
　　I dream and sigh
　　For the days gone by,
Swinging in the grapevine swing.

Out—o'er the water-lilies bonnie and bright,
　Back—to the moss-green trees;
I shouted and laughed with a heart as light
　As a wild rose tossed by the breeze.
The mockingbird joined in my reckless glee,
　I longed for no angel's wing,
I was just as near heaven as I wanted to be,
　Swinging in the grapevine swing.
　　　　　　　　　　—Samuel M. Peck

27

"He Kissed Me in the Rain"

About the only person in Tinyburg who calls the Preacher by his first name is his wife, Carol. Since he's self-conscious about it (Cruden, after *Cruden's Bible Concordance*), he really prefers the more affectionate "Preacher."

For their fifteenth anniversary, Carol and Cruden spent a quiet evening with their three sons, all of whom have biblical names: Mark, Andrew, and David.

Carol fixed a fancy supper and Cruden brought home fresh flowers. After they'd eaten, the five sat around looking at family and wedding photos. After viewing some color slides of the young couple at a party announcing their engagement, Mark asked, "Mom, did you and Daddy fall in love?"

"That's an old-fashioned way of saying it, but yes, your Daddy and I fell in love."

"Is it like falling in the river or something?" continued Mark.

"You do sort of get swept off your feet. Giddy feelings. Floating on clouds."

"Loving someone also means you need that person," Cruden added. "Without each other, you feel incomplete, like a half-person."

"Another question," Mark added. "If you fall *in* love, can you also fall *out* of love, like the baby robins that fell out of our cherry tree?"

Carol replied this time. "Love has its ups and downs. Parents don't float on clouds forever. Your kids get sick. Bills come due. But bad times needn't make you 'fall out' of love, especially if you need each other."

By now David joined in. "Dad, will you and Mom ever fall out of love?"

Swooping him up in the air, Cruden promised, "No one in this family's going to fall out of anything. Now, bedtime!"

Later, Carol asked if she and Mark could drive the car to Bigtown the next day.

"Sure," Cruden said. "I'll look after Andrew and David, and if we need to go somewhere, we'll take the pick-up."

A big back-to-school sale had drawn

mobs of shoppers to the White Oaks Mall.
Carol circled three times to find a parking
space at the far end of Section 2 near their
favorite department store.

She and Mark had fun shopping. "Makes
me feel like I was back in school myself," she
reminisced to her friend, Flo, whom she met
at a lunch counter. Over lunch, Carol said,
"Flo, do you realize what it costs to outfit kids
for school? I need an armored car loaded with
money. And by day's end, a truck to haul everything home."

There were so many bargains that Carol
bought more than she planned, including
Christmas sweaters for Cruden and the boys,
which she put on layaway. She also decided to
get her hair done for Sunday.

By six o'clock, smothered with packages,
they were ready for home. Counting her
money, Carol found only 35¢ in change and a
$1 bill. "Good thing we're finished," she sighed
to Mark. "Here, put this in your pocket toward
next week's allowance."

As they headed toward Section 2 of the
parking lot, distant thunder in the northwest
announced a fast-moving rainstorm. Carol
was glad she parked under a big light, for the
storm brought with it an early dark.

"Hurry," wailed Carol, as she and Mark

pushed two overloaded shopping carts. "It's beginning to sprinkle and our packages will get wet."

By the time they found the car, it was already raining in torrents. Carol, thoroughly soaked, fished around in her purse for her keys. Her hands trembled—they weren't there!

Mark spoke up, "Look, Mom, in the car. You left them in the ignition. We're locked out!"

There was no time to scold herself. "Grab everything and run inside," she cried to Mark. "I'll call your Daddy to bring his keys."

By now, Carol had lost those warm, fuzzy feelings about school days. She wished no one had invented back-to-school sales. Could she ever salvage this waterlogged pile of jeans, gym shorts, sneakers, socks, shirts, jackets, gloves, loose-leaf notebooks, and ball point pens?

Then came the really bad news: she thought her purse was in one of the carts with the packages, but it wasn't. Had she left it on the hood of the car? "Watch everything," she told Mark. "I'll be right back."

She was right back as promised, but no purse. In those few minutes, someone apparently took it. By now she had doubled her wish that back-to-school sales had never been invented.

Trying to be cheerful, Mark said he had the $1.35 she'd given him. But that was little consolation, since her credit cards and driver's license had gone bye-bye in the missing purse.

"Give me the quarter," she said in desperation. "I'll call Cruden."

"Glad you called," Cruden answered. "Been worried—big storm went through, power lines down—"

"Yes, I know all about the storm," she cut in. "Now don't get upset. We're safe here at the mall, but...."

"....but what?"

"I...I locked the keys in the car."

"Carol, if I've told you once, I've told you a hundred times that when you get out of a car always to—"

Carol didn't wait for him to finish. "Save your sermon for Sunday. I need help, not a lecture. Besides, we're soaking wet and hungry."

Cruden softened his tone: "Tell me where you're parked—row 2? I'll be there in about an hour. In the meantime, relax and buy yourselves a nice dinner."

Carol figured she might as well get the

rest of the bad news over with. "But sweetheart, my purse is gone, too, and we're out of money."

Since Cruden prefers bad news in small doses, he decided to end the questioning, promising instead to come as quickly as possible.

Carol looked at Mark, "How much do we have left?"

"The $1 bill and a dime. You spent the quarter to call Daddy."

"A dollar and ten cents—what in the world will that buy for a waterlogged mother and her starving teenager?"

"I saw some candy bars, three for $1. And jumbo bags of corn chips on sale for half price—$1.15 I believe."

"Corn chips would be more filling," Carol said. "Except we're a nickel short. If I weren't too proud, I'd offer $1.10 and see what happens."

Which eventually she did: "I've never begged, but my son's hungry, my keys are locked in the car, I lost my purse, and a dime and $1 bill is all we have. Would you take that for a $1.15 bag of chips?"

The store manager smiled, "Lady, if half of what you say is true, you would deserve the chips for making up the story. Here, take a bag and keep your money."

What luck! Now they could afford two soft drinks. Surrounded by soggy shopping bags, they sat on the edge of a fountain, into which passersby toss coins, as they munched on the corn chips like royalty at a banquet.

Figuring Cruden now had time to be there, mother and son again trudged across the big parking lot, pushing their carts, a light rain still wetting their faces. And Carol's hair was ruined—more money wasted.

They reached the car about the time Cruden and the other two boys arrived in the pick-up. Carol looked through the rain-streaked windshield for a glimpse of Cruden's face. She was relieved to see him wearing an impish little grin, a smile that had won her over the first time she saw him at a high school basketball game.

Rolling down the window, he said he'd pull over and park in the next row. In the few seconds before Cruden was out of the truck and at their side with his keys, Mark whispered, "Look, Mom—the lock button on one of the back doors isn't pushed down."

Sure enough, the button was in its upright position. In her excitement, she'd tried only the front doors.

Carol gingerly backed herself up against the one unlocked door, opened it, pushed down the lock button, then closed it by pushing against it with her body. Too late she realized her skirt was caught in the door, for by now Cruden was at her side. To her surprise and delight, he took her in his arms, gently pushed back the tangled wet hair from her forehead, and kissed her warmly as the rain fell in rivulets down their faces. Suddenly, all the rain-chill in her body was gone.

Then as Cruden turned to unlock the front door on the driver's side, Carol jerked her dress free, coughing repeatedly to cover up the sound of her ripping skirt.

"Carol, you're taking cold in this rain. Hurry, pitch some of your packages in the back of the pick-up and get in the car. I'll follow you in case you get stopped for having no driver's license."

On the thirty-five-mile drive home, the clouds scattered and the setting sun came into view, forming a giant rainbow. Mark said, "You got your wish, Mom. You told Flo you needed a truck to haul our school clothes."

"You can bet I'll never make *that* wish again," she smiled.

After a long silence, Mark spoke again,

"Mom, I saw you push that lock. Wasn't that lying to Daddy?"

Since she thought no one noticed, Mark's question surprised her. She waited a full minute to answer, as if organizing her thoughts: "Mark, I didn't push that button to lie to your Daddy. I pushed it to say I needed him. And I *did* need him. Oh, I wasn't helpless—I could have broken the glass.

"But I needed more than a set of keys. I needed to see his boyish grin. I needed him to hug me like he did and say everything's OK, and, yes, to kiss me in the rain on the parking lot at the mall!

"Most of all, he needed to be needed. An unlocked door would have tattled, 'Carol didn't need you after all.'"

Mark asked, "Is that what you meant last night when you said falling in love is needing someone?"

"When I said that, I had no idea I'd lose my keys today, but yes, it's one example. And so long as we need one another, and meet those needs, we'll see one dark thunderstorm after another melt into a colorful rainbow."

By now their headlights illuminated the driveway as they pulled into home. "Mom," Mark whispered, "if you promise not to tell we mooched chips, I'll not tell you locked the door on purpose."

"Agreed," smiled Carol.

And they never did!

Balm in Gilead

Everyone in the Tinyburg Church knows that chubby little Randy Spiller, age four, is a wiggleworm.

His grandparents, Clay and Edith Barker, know it. Months ago, they gave up trying to keep him quiet, after threatening to tie him with a rope to the end of a pew. His parents, Ted and Candice, know it, because they dropped out of choir for a year so they could sit with him. And Uncle Billy Cutrell, age eighty, knows it, for he sits to one side of the church where he can survey all that goes on. (His nickname's not "Uncle Billy Told-You-So" for nothing.)

But no one dreamed that Randy's antics would trigger a 911 emergency call, right in the middle of the Preacher's sermon.

It began when the Preacher asked Ted and Candice to sing a duet, "There Is a Balm in Gilead," in the morning service, saying "It fits my sermon perfectly."

Ted wondered who would sit with Randy.

"You mean you can't leave him for five minutes?" asked the Preacher.

"Not even one minute."

"Then I've got a solution. My sons, Andrew and Mark, do babysitting for a neighbor. They love kids. We'll put Randy between them, on the second pew from the front. I guarantee they'll keep him still if they have to sit on him."

Randy, who's large for his age, was pleased to sit with the "big boys." When Randy was still a toddler, his grandpa predicted that with his oversize hands, he'd make some baseball team a good catcher: "Look at those fingers, big as a teenager's."

"Oh, Clay," Edith had scolded. "Randy's already too big for his britches, thinks he's another Goliath."

Sunday morning, Ted and Candice sang as sweet a duet as you'd want to hear. Randy, innocent as a Christmas angel, listened in awe:

Sometimes I feel discouraged,
And think my work's in vain,

But then the Holy Spirit
Revives my soul again.

If you cannot preach like Peter,
If you cannot pray like Paul,
Just tell the love of Jesus,
And say He died for all.

There is a balm in Gilead to make the
    wounded whole;
There is a balm in Gilead to heal the sinsick
    soul.

—Author Unknown

"I'm preaching on the balm of Gilead," began the Preacher. "Our word 'balm,' as commonly used, means a fragrant ointment. It also refers to aromatic oils used for healing wounds. In a larger sense, the word includes anything of a soothing nature, such as, 'sleep was a balm to his troubled mind.'

"Balm was prized in Old Testament times, when it was also used to embalm the dead. Some of the finest balm came from Gilead, an area noted for its lush grazing lands, thick forests, and verdant bushes which produced this sweet-smelling and healing oil."

By now, little Randy had heard all he wanted to hear about the balm of Gilead. Itching for new adventures, he stuck his three middle fingers in the little communion cup holder fastened to the pew in front of him. What fun he had, jiggling his fingers up and down, in and out, until Andrew and Mark pulled him back into his seat, remembering their daddy's warning: "No dessert for Sunday dinner if you let Randy squirm around and put on a show."

Meanwhile, the Preacher continued: "As I was saying, balm was a treasure in Bible times. Do you remember when the brothers of Joseph sold him to a caravan of traders for twenty pieces of silver? Those Ishmaelite merchants were en route to Egypt, their camels loaded with spices, balm, and myrrh. Do you suppose they made Joseph walk behind the camels? If so, then on the long journey Joseph probably smelled and was refreshed by the fragrance of the balm of Gilead. Oh, my beloved fellow members, how we need the healing, refreshing touch of a modern-day balm of Gilead in our church."

Little Randy, oblivious to poor Joseph being sold into slavery, eyed the communion cup holder again. Once more he jabbed his fingers into the three little holes. What fun to jiggle them up and down, in and out, so quiet and noiseless that no one noticed.

Since it was a warm, humid day, his little hand grew red and sweaty as he continued to play. Before he realized the danger, Randy pushed his fingers extra hard, so that now they were stuck tightly in the cup holder. The more he pulled, the redder and more swollen his fingers became. Hopelessly locked, he felt like a rabbit, caught in a trap.

Andrew and Mark, sensing an emergency, tugged on Randy's hand until he started to cry. But Mark saved the day by muffling Randy's mouth with a handkerchief. Both brothers then sat ramrod straight and listened to the Preacher as if nothing had happened. The only other witness was Uncle Billy Cutrell, who, as I said earlier, misses nothing.

Out of the corner of his mouth, never taking his eyes off his dad in the pulpit, Andrew whispered to Mark, "I'll keep him quiet—you go find something slick, like grease or hand lotion."

"There's a can of oil in the garage. I'll be right back," replied Mark.

When an usher asked Mark where he was going, he said to get a drink. Instead, he ducked out the back door of the church and crossed the lawn to the pastorium, where he found the can of oil in the garage. He wrapped it carefully inside his Sunday School paper so no one could see.

Returning to his seat, Mark squirted the

lubrication on Randy's chubby fingers, stuck tightly in the cup holders. Little Randy's face, like his chubby fingers, was also flushed and red.

Bad news for all three boys: the oil wouldn't work! Randy, frightened he'd never get free and would have to stay by himself in the church all week like a prisoner in stocks, wanted to cry, but Andrew continued to hold a handkerchief, like a gag, across his mouth.

In desperation, Andrew handed Mark a note. "Go back home and find something else slippery."

"Like what?" whispered Mark.

"Anything—hurry! Mayonnaise, molasses, whatever."

Again an usher questioned Mark, who blamed the sermon on the balm of Gilead for making him thirsty. Crossing the churchyard in record time, he bounded up the steps of the pastorium. He reached in the refrigerator for the mayonnaise, but all he could find was a quart jar, too big to hide under his jacket. Turning to the medicine cabinet, he spied a small, bluish-green bottle of mentholated salve, easy to hide in his pocket.

Trying not to act upset, he marched calmly back down the aisle, sat next to Randy, and quietly opened the bottle of salve and spread a big glob of the oily stuff on the swollen fingers. The salve did little good to free Randy's fingers, but once the lid was opened, the pungent, penetrating odor spread to nearby worshippers, some of whom began to sniffle and clear their throats, or reach for handkerchiefs and tissues to dab at their eyes.

The Preacher, still immersed in his message, had paid no mind to his sons running in and out, nor the opened jar of salve. He was now nearing the conclusion: "Jeremiah the prophet, depressed over the downfall of Israel and Judah, lamented that there was no longer a balm in Gilead, no longer a physician there. Friends, has the balm of Gilead lost its flavor in our lives? Has it evaporated?

"I wish I could describe for you the fragrance of the balm they made in Gilead, centuries ago. Perhaps it resembled the oil of eucalyptus, of menthol, of camphor, of turpentine, all of which you find in modern-day salve.

"And speaking of salve, I remember as a child how my mother rubbed it on me when I had a cold, how its tart odor cleared your nostrils, often brought tears to your eyes. Oh, the power of memory and nostalgia. I feel it now on my feverish chest, the warm flannel, my mother's touch...."

Unaware that a little green bottle of that salve—yes, the genuine product—was exposed on the second pew, its contents generously smeared on Randy's swollen fingers, the Preacher continued: "If I didn't know better, I'd declare someone's opened a bottle of it right here in church. This proves the power of imagination. What I'm smelling right now—or imagine I smell—is identical to that of my boyhood."

Uncle Billy Cutrell, continuing to watch the unfolding saga, decided it was time to act. No way could homemade remedies such as salve free that helpless little boy. He imagined the worst: Andrew pulling so hard he tears the skin off Randy's fingers, who would then scream so loud as to disrupt the entire service, perhaps be traumatized for life, forever feeling insecure and threatened by churches. Who knows—maybe lose all interest in church and the spiritual life? This was a crisis which demanded quick, clear-thinking action.

In the morning paper, he'd read about a new 911 number. The article encouraged readers to lose no time in dialing 911. "Better to call and not need help, than to delay and increase your risk," the paper had warned. Hurrying to the church office, Uncle Billy dialed 911 and pled for a rescue vehicle! (Later, the village board issued him a certificate for being the first citizen in Tinyburg to dial 911.)

Has there ever lived a minister who could keep his wits when the so-called imaginary fragrance of that salve is as pungent as the real thing, and a rescue vehicle pulls up with lights and sirens? Certainly not! And neither could the Preacher.

He stopped his sermon in mid-sentence, stepping aside in mild horror while a fireman in boots and helmet rushed down the aisle with screwdriver and coping saw to free little Randy from the clutches of the cup holder.

Once the excitement died down, Uncle Billy apologized for overreacting and calling 911 to help loosen a couple of half-inch screws: "But how was I to know but what a fire might break out? And little Randy, handcuffed like a prisoner, unable to save his life?"

The morning service never ended—formally, that is. Just sort of dissolved. No closing hymn, no benediction. Andrew and Mark hurried home to put the salve back in the cabinet and the oil in the garage. Grandpa Barker examined Randy's hand, making sure he could still be a big-league ballplayer. Ted and Candice promised each other they'd never sing another duet until Randy was married and settled down, say when he was forty years old, not four.

Then the Preacher rapped for attention:

"One more word. I started out to preach on healing and togetherness, on love and sweet-smelling fragrances. I'm not sure I ever made my point. Maybe my topic was too nebulous. On the other hand, we've had a good time, we've laughed together and recalled old times, some from our childhood. And whoever said it's wrong to laugh in church? To be reminded that we're family?

"We may well remember this service, long after we've forgotten others more formal and precise. Andrew and Mark think they won't get any dessert for dinner. But they will. They were innocent. Randy thinks he'll never get to sit with the big boys again. But he will. Joseph, in the long ago, wearing the chains of slavery, still smelled the balm from Gilead. We, too, in whatever circumstances, can do the same."

He then asked everyone (except Randy, whose fingers were sore) to join hands and sing:

There is a balm in Gilead to make the
    wounded whole;
There is a balm in Gilead to heal the sinsick
    soul.

Jehoshaphat Goes to a Wedding

One of the strangest pictures you'll ever see is on Clay and Edith Barker's piano. It's the wedding picture of their youngest daughter, Kay, when she married Ron Bouton. But instead of holding her bridal bouquet, Kay's holding a cat. Yes, a big, white, alley cat by the name of Jehoshaphat, posing proudly as if he were the star attraction.

"Preposterous!" you say? But anything can happen in Tinyburg, the only city in the United States with an unlisted zip code.

"Now, Kay," advised Edith when they were planning the wedding, "let's have a plain ceremony—pretty, but plain. No heroics, please."

But Kay had other ideas, including a bank

of palms, ferns, and flowers across the entire front of the church: "I want the whole church to look like a garden. And I want the ceremony videotaped."

Since hers was the first wedding video-taped in Tinyburg, it created lots of excitement. Too, it's the best remembered wedding in the history of the Tinyburg Church.

"Let's use two camcorders," suggested Ron, himself an amateur photographer. "One cameraman can stand at the back of the church, which will give us a good video of the soloist, the altar flowers, and the groomsmen as they enter. Another can shoot a video from the front, say standing in the choir, to capture you and your bridesmaids as you come down the aisle."

"A great idea, honey," squealed Kay. "You think of everything. We can edit the two videos into one, giving us a complete movie from both angles, back and front."

Ron engaged Van's Video Service in Big-town to tape the ceremony. Van said he'd do the filming from the back, while his brother-in-law, a slightly overweight fellow named Sonny, stood in the choir and filmed from the front of the church. "Since the ferns and palms will hide Sonny, no one will know he's up there," Van promised.

Sonny arrived well before the organ prelude and sat down on the front row of the choir, behind the flowers. This was probably a mistake. You see, the choir has individual opera seats, the kind with the bottoms that turn up. The problem is that Sonny overestimated the width of the seats. With two extra rolls of videotape in his pockets, his plump body made a tight squeeze when he sat down. But he didn't worry, figuring that when it came time to film, he could suck in his breath and push himself out. Something like a jet pilot hitting the eject button!

During the organ prelude, Sonny glanced at the back side of the pulpit, which was exposed to his view. Inside, curled up asleep, was a big white tomcat.

Sonny thought this was strange, but to the members of the church it wasn't at all unusual.

The tomcat, you see, belongs to Uncle Billy Cutrell, who lives across the street. Uncle Billy calls him Jehoshaphat, named for the fourth king of Judah in the Old Testament.

Jehoshaphat is an excellent mouser. About once a month, when no services are being held, Uncle Billy locks Jehoshaphat inside the church for twenty-four hours or so to chase mice.

Now Jehoshaphat is such a good mouser that he doesn't need a whole day and night to rid the church of rodents. So the rest of the time he curls up inside the pulpit, where it's dark and warm and cozy. Uncle Billy boasts that the reason Jehoshaphat is a religious cat is because he sleeps so close to the altar.

He often jokes, "If some of you back-sliders would come down front where you can hear the Word of God, you might get religion, too. The Bible says in 2 Chronicles 19:4 that King Jehoshaphat brought the people back to God. That's why I named my cat Jehoshaphat. Follow his example, and you'll find the Lord, too!"

By a strange coincidence, the wedding date fell on the day for Jehoshaphat to chase mice. Uncle Billy admits he simply forgot, which explains why on the afternoon of Kay and Ron's wedding, Jehoshaphat was inside the pulpit, sleeping away.

But right now, Sonny, half-wedged in a choir seat, had more to worry about than cats with biblical names. He checked his camcorder, then reviewed the order of service. He was to start filming on the first note of the processional. His orders were to focus his camera through the flowers and ferns, keeping himself out of view of the audience.

The soloist was half-way through "Oh, Promise Me" when Jehoshaphat, apparently wakened by the music, stood up, yawned, and stretched. "Lie back down and be a nice kitty," Sonny whispered. But Jehoshaphat didn't want to lie down. He was curious: "What's going on here?"

Then Sonny patted his knees—"Hop up here, kitty"—which the white cat did. Quickly, Sonny grabbed him and held him securely with both hands until the soloist finished.

When it came time for him to videotape the processional, Sonny wondered what to do with Jehoshaphat. If he got loose and ran down in front, he'd spoil the solemnity of the service. So Sonny decided to hold Jehoshaphat with one hand, using the other to balance the camcorder on his shoulder.

Trying to get up from the choir seat, Sonny discovered he was wedged in tighter than he first imagined. If he braced himself with both hands, he could give a big push and free himself. But first he must turn Jehoshaphat loose, if only for a few seconds.

Those few seconds Sonny needed to free himself was all Jehoshaphat needed to walk down the pulpit steps and start rubbing himself against the legs of the Preacher who was standing in place, waiting for the wedding party. And the cat purred so loudly, that were the organ not playing, you could have heard him at least to the second row of pews, where the mothers of the bride and groom sat.

Sonny realized that although his job was to tape the front view of the wedding, Jehoshaphat was a bigger problem. If left to meander around, he would spoil everything.

Not wishing to be seen, Sonny got down on his stomach under the flowers and candles, in arm's reach of Jehoshaphat. The Preacher, surprised to feel a hand groping around his ankles, turned with a start. Jehoshaphat backed away.

By now the bridesmaids were coming down the aisle. They evidently caught Jehoshaphat's attention, for he started up the aisle toward them, safely out of reach of Sonny's grasp.

Sonny, not to be outdone, determined to crawl down the aisle after Jehoshaphat. None of the wedding guests saw him, for by now everyone had stood and turned, facing the back of the sanctuary where the bride was about to make her entry.

It's now or never, Sonny said to himself as he crawled between the Preacher's legs in pursuit of Jehoshaphat, now even with the third row of pews. For some unknown but providential reason, Jehoshaphat abruptly turned aside and hid under a pew in row three. Still crawling on his knees, Sonny caught up with Jehoshaphat and grabbed him with both hands. But alas, he had left his camera in the choir loft with no way to retrieve it.

So Sonny just lay there under a pew, holding Jehoshaphat until the ceremony ended.

Van, videotaping from the rear of the church, was one of the few who saw what happened. And yes, he saw it all through the lens of his camera, because it recorded everything! It was like a bad movie that wouldn't end. His reputation was ruined—Van's Video Service would never get another job in Tinyburg!

After the ceremony, the guests assembled in the church basement for the reception where Clay, the bride's father, set up a large television. "I want to preview the video right now," he said. "Some of the guests may never have another chance to see it."

Although the truth was that some didn't care for a first chance to view it, Clay beamed with pride as he turned on the set.

"Daddy, the video taken from the front of the church first," Kay cried. "I want to see the processional, me walking down the aisle on your arm."

But there was no "front" video. Sonny had spent the entire wedding on the floor, chasing and holding Jehoshaphat.

"There must be *some* explanation," wailed Kay when told the first video was blank. "We agreed on two cameras, one at the back and one in the choir."

"Don't worry," interrupted Van. "Let's see the one video made from the back. You can still see your faces during the recessional."

The opening sequence, in full color, was stunning. The acolytes lighting the candles. The luxuriant bank of flowers, ferns, and palms across the front. The soloist, poised and smiling. The minister, the groom, and the groomsmen, entering from a side door. Now for the processional, even if it showed only the backs of the bridal party.

But no! What's that rubbing against the Preacher's leg? A cat? What is this, a joke? And that—whatever it is—yes, a grown man, on hands and knees, grabbing for the cat but missing, now crawling up the aisle in pursuit, finally lying on the floor between rows two and three!

But cameras don't lie. It happened the way the video said it did.

If you know the Barker family, you are aware that although they're exact and precise, moving through life with an air of "class," they can also laugh and enjoy fun, even at their own expense. Clay began laughing first, then Edith, then the newlyweds, Kay and Ron. Now everyone joined in, even the embarrassed cameramen, Van and Sonny.

In fact, when friends recall the Barker-Bouton wedding, what they remember best is not the beautiful gowns the girls wore or the banks of flowers. Instead, they remember Jehoshaphat, the uninvited guest.

After the cake was cut, the gifts opened, and Kay had thrown her bouquet and garter to well-wishers, the party went back upstairs for a formal portrait. On an impulse, Kay grabbed Jehoshaphat, now nibbling on a piece of wedding cake.

"Kay, you're not posing with that alley cat here in the sanctuary!" cried Edith.

"Yes, mother," Kay replied. "How else could we convince our children and grand-children that Jehoshaphat was an honored guest?"

So that's how Jehoshaphat weaseled into the picture. And if you don't believe me, go visit Clay and Edith in Tinyburg. Look for yourself—the picture's on their piano.

Ever since, Uncle Billy makes certain that when there's a wedding, Jehoshaphat is safe at home. But he still enjoys kidding his friends, "If you backsliders would sit down by the pulpit, you might get in the movies. In fact, you might get religion, too, just like Jehoshaphat!"

Licorice Climbs a Tree

"Help! I'm falling!"

Candice Spiller was loading the drier when she heard Randy's cry. Running outside, she saw him clinging to the top of their sycamore tree, trying to rescue Licorice, their cat.

Cupping her hands, she hollered, "You're OK. Just scoot down, slow and easy."

"I'm scared," Randy cried, clutching a limb with one arm and the other around Licorice. "It's scary up here."

"Then stay put while I bring a ladder."

Instead she ran inside and dialed Ted's work number at the Country Grain Elevator: "Come home quick—Randy's stuck in our sycamore tree—too high for our stepladder."

The story of Randy in the tree begins on

his birthday last summer, the year he got his first two-wheel bicycle. His daddy even helped him pick out a pair of biker pants, the snug-fitting style that bike racers wear.

His sisters made fun of the color—a bright, florescent orange with big black polka dots. "Your pants are funny," Rhonda teased. "I bet they glow in the dark."

Randy didn't mind—he likes bright colors. Randy also likes their eighty-year-old neighbor, Uncle Billy Cutrell. Whenever any Spiller kid has a birthday, Uncle Billy brings a sack of candy. This year, for Randy, it was licorice-flavored jelly beans.

"Ugh!" said Randy. "They taste icky."

"Is that the way to thank Uncle Billy?" scolded Candice.

"I should have known better," apologized Uncle Billy. "Most kids today have never heard of licorice. When I was a boy, we bought it in long, chewy strips, either red or black. When I found these jelly beans with that flavor, I guess I reverted to my boyhood."

"I like licorice," volunteered Ruthie, Randy's other sister. "I'll eat them."

Randy, now deciding he did like licorice, ran to hide the sack in a corner of his bedroom closet. No way would his sisters eat his jelly beans.

A few evenings later a stray kitten showed up at the Spillers. "Can we keep him?" asked the children.

When their parents agreed, Ruthie begged to pick out a special name, "Something no one ever heard of."

"What about Licorice?" suggested Randy, remembering his birthday treat. So Licorice it was.

Licorice had one bad habit—he was forever climbing something. He climbed on furniture, utility poles, small trees, fences, street signs, and clotheslines. One morning during breakfast the youngsters heard the pitifulest cry. Licorice had climbed the rose trellis, then leaped onto the roof. Afraid to come down, he was crying. Randy quickly put a stepladder next to the lower end of the roof and coaxed Licorice to safety.

"Someday that cat's going to climb to the moon, and that will be the end of that!" predicted Candice.

"Oh, Mom, cats can't jump to the moon," teased Rhonda.

"I got my metaphors mixed," she admitted, thinking of the nursery rhyme:

Hey diddle diddle,
The cat and the fiddle,
The cow jumped over the moon;

The little dog laughed
To see such a sport,
And the dish ran away with the spoon.

And so passed the summer, the girls dressing Licorice in little doll clothes, rescuing him from high places, and Randy endlessly riding his two-wheeler all over Tinyburg, wearing his orange and polka-dot racer pants.

"Son, if you ever get lost, someone's sure to find you with those florescent racing shorts," his dad said, laughing.

This was the same summer that Candice sometimes noticed a faraway look in Ted's eyes when they'd be sitting in the Tinyburg Church. Ted was worrying about one of his best customers at the Country Grain Elevator, a young farmer. He was a hard-working, ambitious fellow who had lost his arm in a hay-bailer. It happened right after he had mortgaged his farm to buy some more acreage and a lot of expensive machinery. The accident forced him to sell his farm and let the machinery go back at a big loss. Ted wondered why God let this happen to such a promising young father.

Finally, Ted confided with the Preacher. "Sometimes I feel God's a million miles away. I can't pray like I did. Do you really think God has anything to do with what happens here on earth?"

"Ted, I wish I had an easy answer. At times we must trust, even when there's little to believe in."

"I don't understand, Preacher."

"Remember the man in the Bible who asked Jesus to heal his son? When Jesus told him to have faith, the father replied, 'Lord, I believe; help thou mine unbelief.'"

Ted asked how you can believe when there's nothing there to believe with.

The Preacher opened his Bible to Galatians 4:9. "But now, after ye have known God, or rather *are* known of God" (author's italics).

"What's the point?" asked Ted.

"The point is that God sees *us* before we see *Him*. God believes in us, maybe more than we believe in ourselves. Jesus taught that not one sparrow falls to the ground without God knowing."

The day after this conversation Ted's phone rang, telling him Randy was stuck in a tree.

"Tell him to hold on," he ordered Candice. "I'll be home in three minutes."

Once Ted was home, Candice filled in the details: "When Licorice got stranded in the treetop, Randy scooted after him. But when he looked down and saw how far it was to the ground, he lost his nerve, too—just froze."

Ted threw off his jacket and started up the tree. "Steady, boy, don't move, don't look down, stay where you are."

By now Ted could see Randy's bright orange biker pants through the leaves, and yes, Licorice, too, eyes wide with fright.

But when he was within three feet of Randy, Ted saw he couldn't go any higher. The limb Randy was clutching had a rotten place in it. If he put his weight on it, too, all of them would fall.

So he tried to coax Randy from where he was. "Easy, son, back yourself down, step at a time. I'm here, almost close enough to touch you." But Randy wouldn't budge. Fear paralyzed him. His fingers were white from gripping the limb, as if coated with ice.

"Call the rescue squad," Ted hollered down to Candice, trying to keep as calm as if he were ordering a pizza. "They'll think of something. I'll stay up here with Randy."

The rescue squad first considered a long ladder to the top of the tree, but decided the weight might topple the rotting limb. So they unloaded a firemen's net from their truck, hoping they could persuade Randy to jump.

Once the net was in position, Ted told

Randy to turn loose and jump, taking Licorice, too. "You'll fall through the leaves right into the net. You can't miss. The men on the ground are your friends."

"But Dad, I can't see the net for the leaves. How do I know anyone's down there? I can't Dad, I can't turn loose."

"Randy, Randy, now listen," shouted one of the rescue squad men who overheard him. "Maybe you can't see our net, but I see someone up there wearing a pair of bright-orange shorts with polka dots. Any idea who that might be?"

"It's me," sobbed Randy.

"Then jump, even if you're blind. So long as we see you, that's all that matters. Trust us...now jump!"

"Okay, here I come!"

And with that, he turned loose, tumbling through the leaves and branches to the safety of the net. Licorice looked around as if to say, "What's all the excitement?" then calmly walked over to his feeding pan for a late supper.

The rest of the Spiller family didn't take it so calmly. Rhonda, Ruthie, and Randy were all talking at once, retelling every detail. "I'd have been scared, too," admitted Rhonda. "Maybe stayed up there my whole life."

"I was scared, too," admitted Randy. "Real scared. But when a fireman said he saw me, even if I couldn't see him, I knew I was okay. So I held Licorice real tight and turned loose. And here I am!"

Ted thought about the sparrows falling from heaven, about God knowing us before we know him, seeing us when we can't see him. Too, he remembered his friend who lost his land as well as an arm. And he said a prayer for him, that he, too, would fall safely into the net of God's care.

Then, like a heavenly phone call, Ted heard an inner voice, "I need someone to help hold the net." Which explains why that very afternoon he went to the home of the embattled young farmer, where they talked long into the night about possible solutions.

When Ted said goodnight, his friend thanked him for bringing the best of all gifts— the gift of hope and faith.

Close the Gate Behind You

When Rhonda Spiller came home from school with a bad report card in reading, her parents, Candice and Ted, said no television for a month!

"Not even the cartoons on Saturday?" complained Rhonda. "I think that's cruel."

"It may be cruel, but that's the way it is," replied Candice. "Poor grades mean no television, especially poor grades in reading."

The first Saturday that Rhonda couldn't watch cartoons, she was so restless she made the whole family miserable. Standing by the cage where their pet parrot, Casper, was pruning himself, she mocked, "Nothing to do! Nothing to do! Nothing to do!"

And Casper, who's the smartest parrot in

Tinyburg and maybe the whole world, joined in the chorus, "Nothing! Nothing! Nothing!"

Candice broke out laughing. "What a tragedy! My poor, little, underprivileged girl has nothing to do, and my parrot has nothing to say but nothing. So nothing it will be. Nothing for lunch, nothing for television, nothing to read or play, nothing, nothing, nothing. Let's all have one big nothing day and cry a dishpan of tears."

Other mothers in the neighborhood envy Candice because she can act like a clown in the worst of times. When she can't scold her kids out of mischief, she can joke them out of it. Her magic worked again; Rhonda broke into a big grin.

"Then can I go to Grandma's?"

Candice said yes, if she'd leave her frown at home. "I keep warning you that frown is going to freeze on your face someday, making you so ugly no one will ever look at you again."

Since Grandma Edith Barker lives just around the corner and two blocks down the street, Rhonda was there in minutes.

Grandma Edith hugged her and asked how long she could stay. "As long as I please," Rhonda replied. "There's nothing to do at home, not even television. Grandma, was your mother ever mean to you and turned off the TV?"

"Child, there was no television to turn off when I was your age. Only two of our neighbors owned a radio. I was married and thirty years old when I saw my first television program."

"Weren't you bored?"

"Oh, there was plenty to do. We didn't know what television was, so we didn't miss it. We entertained ourselves, rather than depending on someone else."

"What do you mean?" asked Rhonda.

"I mean that most television is watching someone else sing or perform or play football. Don't get me wrong—within reason, TV's fun to watch, and we see the news and all that. But if you spend all your time watching someone else have a good time, you miss home-made fun with your family and friends."

"Grandma, it's always happy time with you."

"Maybe that's because I spoil you. But don't ask to watch cartoons. I wouldn't go around your parents."

"You say the funniest things, Grandma, like 'going around your parents.'"

"It means that we obey your parents' rules at my house, the same as if you were at home."

"Then if I can't watch cartoons, would you tell me another story about when you were a little girl?"

Edith promised she would, soon as she washed a pan of apples. "I'm making sliced apple pies for Sunday dinner," she smiled. "Let's sit on the back porch, and while I peel apples, I'll tell you a story.

"It's been seventy years since I was your age," Edith began. "Life was so different then. So many people lived on small family farms. Every half mile or so, you'd see a farmhouse, barn, feed lot, garden, and chicken house.

"We were practically self-sufficient. Mother—that was your great-grandmother— she sewed most of our clothes. If roads were muddy in the winter, we had plenty to eat without going to the store. Daddy smoked our bacon and hams, and mother canned sausage and soup mix. We buried turnips in the ground and covered them with straw to keep them from freezing. Our shelves were filled with all kinds of canned fruit and vegetables, our own popcorn, dried apples, both kinds of potatoes. Plus fresh milk and eggs from our cows and chickens."

"Wasn't that a lot of work?" asked Rhonda, reaching for a slice of red apple.

"Looking back, yes. At the time, we didn't

know any difference. That's why we didn't miss TV. There was so much to do and see. But it wasn't all work. We had the woods and fields to walk in, wild flowers to pick, nuts to gather, creeks to wade in, and long, snowy hills for sledding."

"Was your mother ever mean to you, like my Mom who said I couldn't watch cartoons today?"

"Now Rhonda," replied her grandmother, sternly, almost scolding. "You've asked me that once. Because Candice said no TV doesn't make her a mean mother. If she didn't care about you, she'd let you watch anything, go everywhere, and never show any interest in your grades.

"But back to my mother, yes, she and Daddy upset me if I couldn't have my way. But they didn't deserve to be called mean."

"How did they upset you?"

"For one thing, Mother was always reminding me to close this gate or that door. I got so tired of her saying, 'Now Edith, close the gate behind you.' Or, 'Edith, shut the door— don't let the cold air inside.'

"On our family farm, I guess we had a dozen gates. If we left the gate open to the chicken yard, they got out and scratched up the garden. If we failed to close the pasture gate, the cattle wandered off. If we left the pig pen open, the pigs ran out in the yard and rooted up the grass. If we left the barn door open on cold nights, the sheep got out.

"So it was always 'Close the gate, Edith,' or 'Shut the door behind you, Edith.' I never intended to leave those gates open. Mother seemed obsessed. I got to where I'd mimic her, so Daddy could hear, for he was hung up on that gate business, too. Only I didn't say it in a nice way—sort of mocked them, imitating the way they said it."

"Did you get spanked?"

"Goodness no. They thought it was funny, unless we had company, when they'd look at me real straight, and I knew to stop.

"When I got older, I asked Mother why she worried so much about gates and doors.

"She said it all had a deeper meaning, that she believed in leaving things in good order. Like if you were a guest in someone's home, you made up your bed the next morning and wiped the lavatory and cleaned the mirror. She said it was bad manners to go home and leave things in a mess behind you.

"She reminded me that people who run through gates and never shut them or chase out a door and never bother to close it are thinking only of themselves. They ignore the comfort of those still in the house on cold days, or the safety of animals which might wander away and get hurt."

Rhonda said she wished she had known her great-grandmother and listened while she scolded Edith.

"I do, too. She lived to be quite old but died before you were born. She was a wonderful woman."

Rhonda asked how she died.

"Sort of faded away. Nothing like cancer or a stroke. Just wore out. I remember how depressed she was after Daddy died. We tried our best to move her into town. But she wouldn't budge from the farm. Said it was home to her, although she did give up her chickens and garden. But one thing she never gave up."

"What was that?" asked Rhonda.

"She *never* stopped talking about gates. There was this one big gate when you pulled in her drive off the highway. We told her she didn't need that gate. Whoever came to visit had to get out and open it. She said it gave her something to do, locking up each night before she went to bed.

"One day I drove out to see her. Usually I'd call, but this time I didn't, just surprised her. But she surprised me. She had hired a woman to clean her house. I mean clean house the old-fashioned way, a room at a time. It was like war. Took up every rug, scrubbed and waxed the floors, aired the bedding, cleaned all the windows, washed every dish and pot and pan in the kitchen, painted the bathroom walls.

"I said, 'Mother, what in the world are you doing? Your house is not that dirty. And why didn't you let me help?' She didn't answer and I didn't argue. In a sense, I was relieved. Figured she was getting a new lease on life after Daddy died. Was coming back to reality, taking pride in how her house looked. But I was wrong."

"How were you wrong?"

"In a few days, Mother slipped back into her old routine of not seeming to care about living. Didn't eat properly. I told her how disappointed I was, that I thought this spurt of house cleaning marked a turning point.

"She said no, she was preparing to close the gate for the last time."

Rhonda, wide-eyed, asked if that meant she was locking herself in for good.

Edith explained, "She meant her hunch that she was going to die. She wanted to leave everything in order, nothing out of place, no dirt or clutter or muss anywhere."

"Did that make you sad?" asked Rhonda, who now had tears in her eyes.

"Yes, very sad. However, I knew Mother wanted it that way, and I was glad for her that she had time to set her house in order, as she called it, instead of going suddenly with work left undone."

"Did she die that day?"

"Oh, no. She lived several weeks, but she was never really sick. Finally, over her objections, we moved her to the hospital. The last afternoon we were together, she made me promise to go by the house and check on things. I kissed her goodbye and turned to leave. She raised her hand as if to signal me, 'And Edith, remember to close the gate when you leave...yes, the gate to the driveway.'"

Rhonda could only whisper, "Did you close the gate like you promised?"

"Certainly. I never left a gate open in my life! Why would I then? But Rhonda, those were her last words to me. That night, she passed away in her sleep."

Edith reached for the tail of her apron to wipe the tears that had splashed on her glasses. Then to Rhonda, "I know you're upset with your Mom about the television, like I was upset about my mother and all those gates on the farm. But your Mom and my mother were giving us the same message, in different words. Each was saying, 'Be considerate of others; keep your life in order; be responsible for your little corner of the world. Turn off the TV now and then; always close the gate; take the long look, the courteous look. Most of all, don't make a mess of your life—and don't leave a mess behind you."

Froggie Went A-Courtin'

Clay and Edith Barker made it plain they didn't want—repeat, didn't want—a reception on their fiftieth wedding anniversary.

"But, Mother," argued Candice. "A golden anniversary comes only once."

"I don't care," replied Edith. "I've seen too many and they're all the same. Cake and punch, corsages, posing for pictures, receiving line."

"Yes, and your friends had rather be somewhere else, but they come out of courtesy," added Clay.

"Clay, you don't want to admit you're getting older," joined in Ted.

"You're wrong there," replied Clay, putting his arm around Edith's waist. "I'm just proud the good Lord let us live this long together. Lots of married couples never make it this far. But a fancy reception, no!"

"Okay, then," suggested Candice. "If Ted and I think up something different, say on the light side, would you go along?"

They thought a minute, then nodded, "Okay, so long as it's not the same cookie-and-punch routine."

That night Ted and Candice held a family council with their teenage daughters, Rhonda and Ruthie. "We have three months to get ready," Candice explained. "Let's make this an anniversary Tinyburg will never forget. First, we'll learn more about Mother and Dad's courtship, little secrets they've never told."

Rhonda and Ruthie volunteered for the job.

"Grandma Edith, what did you and Grandpa do on dates and how did he pop the question?" asked Ruthie when she and Rhonda stopped by after school.

"Why do you ask?" joked Clay. "Already thinking about getting engaged, and you only fifteen?"

"Oh, Grandpa," said Rhonda. "Can't you be serious about anything?"

"That was more than fifty years ago," explained Edith. "Life's so different now. We didn't have television and other entertainment. Both of us lived on farms, and our recreation was mainly picnics, church socials, and the like.

"Clay and I had been dating nearly a year. You wouldn't believe it now, but Clay was so shy. I thought he'd never propose. But he finally did, on our way home from a church social."

"Did the party—or social, as you call it—did it have a romantic theme that put Grandpa in the mood?" asked Rhonda.

"Sort of. At parties, we'd sing ourselves hoarse. Mainly folk songs, handed down from other generations. That night we sang 'Froggie Went A-Courtin'. I guess we sang it a hundred times."

"Froggie went a-what?" asked Ruthie, a question mark in her voice.

"It's a silly tune about a frog who courted—that means dating—a mouse. When Froggie proposed, Miss Mousie needed permission from her uncle, a rat. The song describes the wedding supper in a hollow tree where a bumblebee played a banjo, and a black cat barged in and ate Miss Mousie!"

"At her own wedding supper?" gasped Ruthie.

"Remember I said it was a silly song. Want to hear a few verses?

>Froggie went a-courtin' and he did ride,
>Uh-huh.

Froggie went a-courtin' and he did ride
With a sword and a pistol by his side,
  Uh-huh.

He rode up to Miss Mousie's door, Uh-huh.
He rode up to Miss Mousie's door
He knocked so hard he made it roar, Uh-huh.

Miss Mousie asked him to come in, Uh-huh.
Miss Mousie asked him to come in—
The way they courted was a sin, Uh-huh.

He took Miss Mousie on his knee, Uh-huh.
He took Miss Mousie on his knee
And said, "Miss Mousie, will you marry me?"
  Uh-huh.

"The song describes Miss Mousie asking consent from Mr. Rat, Mr. Rat buying her a wedding gown, and the nuptial supper in a hollow tree."

Clay broke in. "Let me sing a verse":

What shall the wedding supper be? Uh-huh.
What shall the wedding supper be?
Two red beans and a black-eyed pea,
  Uh-huh.

First came in was a bumble-bee, Uh-huh.
First came in was a bumble-bee
With his banjo on his knee, Uh-huh."

—Author Unknown

"Grandpa, we didn't know you could sing that good?"

"Singer or no singer, I'm stopping before the verse that tells how a big cat appears at the supper and eats Miss Mousie, leaving Mr. Froggie a widower, as he puts it!"

Edith picked up the story: "On our way home from the party, Clay twisted and fumbled, cleared his throat, and finally said, 'Edith, if I'll be your Froggie, will you be my Mousie?'"

Clay blushed. "Now Edith, you didn't need to tell that!" Rhonda and Ruthie thought it hilarious.

"Our wedding itself, well, it was very plain. We slipped off on a Friday night to the preacher's house, never said 'Boo' to our parents. It was June 3 and the strawberries were ripe. Our country pastor raised a big garden— had to, because we paid him so little. His specialty was strawberries, big, juicy, red ones. Hardly needed sugar.

"His family was eating supper when we knocked, since they didn't know we were coming. We told them to finish their meal, but the preacher said they were through except dessert, and he'd marry us right then. So he did, with his family looking on."

"No music, no flowers, no ring-bearers, no reception?" asked Ruthie.

"None of that. Just tied the knot and said 'God bless you!'"

"After the ceremony, the preacher's wife insisted we stay for dessert. My, was it good! Strawberry shortcake, made in a deep crock. Nobody in the community could make short-cake like she did. She rolled homemade pie dough out in big, thin sheets, which she baked to a crisp brown in the oven. Then she mashed and sweetened the berries, broke the crust in pieces, and layered it in the deep crock."

"My mother made shortcake with a soft biscuit dough," added Clay. "But since that night, I've insisted on shortcake with pie crust, the old-fashioned way."

"I'm sentimental, too," added Edith. "For when June rolls around and the strawberries ripen, I fantasize that Clay and I are in our twenties again, enjoying shortcake with that farmer-preacher and his family."

"No wonder you make so many short-cakes!" said Rhonda.

When the girls reported to Candice and Ted, Candice's eyes sparkled. "We'll surprise Mother and Daddy with a froggie-mousie re-ception on their anniversary!"

"A froggie-mousie what?" asked Ted, who remembered the year Candice commandeered live circus animals for the Christmas pageant.

"No real animals," promised Candice. "Only make believe! Mother and Daddy turned everything over to me, so I'm going to dress them in frog and mouse costumes."

"You'll never get them inside the church dressed like that," warned Ted.

"Oh, they won't know about it until the day of the reception. And Ted, I'll dress you like the big black cat, and Rhonda, you be the rat, and Ruthie the bumblebee. I'll rent costumes at a theatrical supply house in Bigtown. I can't wait!"

Ted urged caution, but Rhonda and Ruthie outvoted him.

They decorated the basement walls of the Tinyburg Church with big cutouts of mice, frogs, cats, and bumblebees. At first, Clay and Edith balked at putting on their costumes. "You wanted something different," argued Candice. "So be good sports and enjoy yourselves."

At the reception, the guests were amused at the funny costumes. "What's this?" wondered Uncle Billy Cutrell. "A Halloween party in June? And where's the cake and punch?"

Candice, adjusting the antennae on Ruthie the bumblebee, didn't bother to answer.

"If anyone except Candice planned this, I'd be shocked," observed Aunt Sarah Biggs. "You can't outguess that girl. It wouldn't surprise me some Sunday to find the church-house turned upside down, the roof resting on the foundation."

Candice introduced what she called the "Barker-Spiller Theatrical Troupe." Edith played the role of Miss Mousie, Clay was Mr. Froggie, Ted was the Black Cat, Rhonda was Uncle Rat, and Ruthie wore the Bumblebee costume, complete with antennae.

What they did was sing "Froggie Went A-Courtin'," acting out the parts. It was hilarious. And yes, different! Miss Grace, a spinster, whispered to Aunt Sarah that if it took that kind of shenanigans to snare a husband, she'd continue in unmarried bliss!

For refreshments—can you guess? Candice and her helpers carried out big crocks from the church kitchen, filled with old-fashioned strawberry shortcake, made with the recipe from their wedding supper fifty years ago.

Each guest enjoyed a generous helping, and no one seemed bashful to come back for seconds, until every one of the big serving bowls was as empty as a Christmas stocking on December 26. By now, Clay and Edith had unwound and had the time of their lives.

At the end, Clay gave an impromptu speech. "We overlooked one thing—the last verse of the frog song."

"Sing it!" shouted Uncle Billy, sparking a round of applause. Which Clay did:

There's pen and ink all on the shelf, Uh-huh.
There's pen and ink all on the shelf
If you want any more, you can write it
    yourself, Uh-huh!

"I'm not here to sermonize," Clay continued. "But that last verse tells me that each person has a hand in writing his own life story. It's largely up to us whether we fail or succeed, make a mess of things or do what's decent. Marriage is that way. Me and Edith, well, we made our own way, wrote our own story, fifty verses in all up 'till now. And hopefully, more to come. When we promised to take each other for better or worse, we meant 'worse' as well as better. We never thought of divorce—oh, a time or two, I did consider murder!

"Edith brags about the shortcake the preacher's wife served. I also remember the advice that old country preacher gave us while we ate.

"He said there's a difference in a wedding and a marriage. You can condense a wedding ceremony to about three minutes, but a marriage takes a lifetime. He also said no married couple's ever been known to 'live happily ever after.' Most of us live 'bumpily' ever after, but the bumps help us appreciate the broad, smooth places. He said marriage isn't so much *finding* the right person as *becoming* the right person. Edith and I have learned that although some marriages are made in heaven, they must be lived here on earth.

"I'm sure that country preacher never took a course in marriage counseling, but he gave me and Edith a big dose of common sense, plus a generous serving of strawberries from his garden."

As the guests said goodbye to Clay and Edith and headed to their homes in Tinyburg, many were humming:

> He took Miss Mousie on his knee, Uh-huh.
> He took Miss Mousie on his knee
> And said, "Miss Mousie, will you marry me?"
>   Uh-huh.

They also took with them beautiful memories of strawberry shortcakes, bumps in the road, sweethearts and singalongs, plus the magic and mystery of marriage.

Ted's Nativity Scene

Although Ted Spiller's not much of a hammer and nail fellow, he's a genius in putting others to work, a real detail man. In the Tinyburg Church, his organizational skills fit him perfectly for chairman of the Outreachers. This is a group of volunteers who do minor repairs for elderly members and widows. Nothing major. Little jobs such as leaky faucets, clogged gutters, frozen water pipes, and broken windows. Ted schedules the jobs, buys the materials, and assigns the volunteers as needed.

At Christmas, the Outreachers build a manger scene on the church lawn. It's not as big a job as some think, for Ted came up with the idea of a permanent creche that's dismantled each year and stored in his garage.

He drew a diagram and assigned a code number to each piece of the creche, making it much easier to assemble.

Once the creche is in place, the church youth haul in bales of straw, put up floodlights, connect a tape deck for background music, borrow one or two live animals, and set the mannequins in place—Joseph, Mary, the Wise Men, and baby Jesus. Some years the youth dress as Bible characters and make it a living nativity scene.

Ted takes special delight when the youth play the roles of Mary, Joseph, and the shepherds. Live actors give an authentic look to the creche and attract larger crowds of spectators. Ted's tried—without success—to put a newborn baby in the manger.

Candice scolded him. "No mother in her right mind would expose a three- or four-day-old infant to the night air, let alone put a baby in the care of teenagers!" But Ted never stopped dreaming.

On the last Sunday in November, Ted put a notice in the church bulletin for volunteers to be at the church by nine a.m. on Saturday, December 2. "I'll lay out the materials on the lawn," he added, "and by noon the creche will be finished."

Sunday afternoon, Aunt Sarah Biggs, teacher of the ladies' Bible class, called Ted:

"See you're getting ready to put up the creche next Saturday. Say, Ted, I've got another good deed for your Outreachers."

"How's that?"

"My neighbors—you know, the ones with three kids—well, she's expecting another one about Christmas. Don't think they exactly planned it that way, which is none of my business. Anyway, they're crowded for room, and he hasn't worked much since last summer. He's a carpenter, and construction work has been slow."

"They don't attend our church, do they?" Ted inquired.

"No, but that's beside the point. The reason I'm calling is they need help. Two weeks ago, the father started to convert their garage into another bedroom. Planned to do the work himself. Then he turned his ankle, bad sprain, all swollen. No broken bones, but he's behind schedule, and I don't think he can finish that bedroom before cold weather and the baby get here."

"I see," said Ted.

"But Ted, we've got to do more than *see*. This is an open door for your Outreachers. With enough help, you could do that whole job next Saturday. Give them time to paint and paper before the baby comes."

"That would be nice, Aunt Sarah. But our little group of volunteers doesn't tackle big jobs, and we give preference to the needs of our own members. Besides, Saturday is the day to put up the Christmas creche."

"Couldn't you do both?" asked Aunt Sarah, not easily discouraged. "Or maybe postpone the creche for another week?"

Ted, committed to a full schedule for all of December, grew impatient. He bristled that a seventy-year-old woman with no children to look after could think of so many jobs for busy fathers like himself. He didn't say so out loud, but he did remind Aunt Sarah that he had all he could manage in December without converting a garage into a bedroom for a needy family:

"You've got wiring and plumbing and heating and roofing and windows and doors and... Aunt Sarah, I just can't do it. I owe something to my own family. It happens every Christmas—we get caught up doing this, doing that, going here, going there; we wear out and talk cross with our families; we overspend and overeat, and then whoosh! It all explodes in our face!"

"I know, Ted," she agreed. "Some Christmases, I've gone over my head, too. So here's an alternate suggestion: forget the creche on the church lawn this year and do the bedroom instead."

"Not put up the creche!" he replied in horror. "You mean leave Mary and Joseph and the baby and the Wise Men stored in my garage? What kind of Christmas would that be?"

"I don't know, Ted. I just know a hard-working family needs a roof over their heads for the holidays."

Candice, hearing the conversation, reminded Ted that if he could line up a few more volunteers, one crew could assemble the creche while a second crew, under his direction, worked on the bedroom.

"Yes, and with a little imagination, I could be Santa Claus for all of Tinyburg, carrying around a big bag with something for everyone. But I'm not Santa Claus, and I've a mind not to do either one, creche or bedroom. And that's that!"

But "that" was not "that," for before the evening service, Ted changed his mind. He asked the Preacher for time to make an announcement, then repeated Aunt Sarah's appeal for donated labor to convert a garage to a bedroom. "But friends, I can't manage the creche, too. So I suggest we skip the manger scene this year and put all our energies into adding that room for Sarah's neighbors."

A chorus of amens swelled up from the congregation, and the following Saturday morning, a work crew twice its normal size showed up at Aunt Sarah's neighbors. Ted arrived early, mapping out who was to do what, consulting with the young carpenter-father where this door was to go, the number of electrical outlets, how big an opening to leave for the front picture window. As I said, Ted's no hammer-and-nail man. But he's a genius at details!

Anyone who didn't see those men work couldn't believe they finished the bedroom by dark. They even painted the outdoor trim and the indoor woodwork. Only the wallpaper was lacking.

But Monday morning, George and Mae Hunter took care of that. George, a blind paperhanger, and his wife, Mae, who moves the ladders and does the pasting, donated their time and hung the prettiest nursery paper you ever saw: bright red toy soldiers with muskets and drums, on a white background. Matching the colorful paper was no problem to George, in spite of his blindness. "Trade secret," he smiled, when Aunt Sarah asked how he did it.

When Aunt Sarah's Sunday school class

held their Christmas party, they substituted a baby shower for their traditional gift exchange. "Us old ladies have more knickknacks than we've got room for," noted one of the members. "Did me good to shop for baby things."

The carpenter's wife had her baby on December 22, a seven-pound two-ounce boy, whom they named Teddy! This pleased the parents, as they now had two boys and two girls.

Mother and baby came home from the hospital on Christmas Eve. As an added surprise, the youth of Tinyburg Church moved the Mary and Joseph mannequins from Ted's garage, borrowed a couple of sheep from a farmer, hauled in two bales of hay, set up floodlights, and played recorded music.

All this they did—not on the lawn of the Tinyburg Church—but in front of the picture window of the new bedroom! On an impulse, one teenager ran home for a string of red and green twinkly lights which he strung around the picture window like a festive frame of color.

After supper, the young couple placed Teddy, the new baby, in a bassinet near the window so he could be seen by passersby. As word of mouth spread, cars and vans from all over Tinyburg, and even from Pretense, seven miles north, began to circle the block. Many parked their vehicles and stood on the lawn, gazing at the most beautiful manger scene ever displayed in Tinyburg, one with a living, two-day old baby! It being dark, some onlookers even allowed tears to trickle down their cheeks, which in daylight they would have quickly brushed aside self-consciously.

"Oh, Daddy," shouted Ruthie Spiller, who was five years old that Christmas. "Let's put the creche in front of someone's house every Christmas instead of at the church. And use a real baby."

"In a small village like Tinyburg, there might not always be a new baby the third week in December."

"Then you and Mommy can have one every Christmas so I'll have lots and lots of brothers and sisters!"

"You're talking about a baby factory, not Christmas!" smiled Ted. "Some people in Tinyburg already think I'm Santa Claus. But don't expect a miracle every year!"

With that, he swept little Ruthie in his arms, kissed her, and whispered, "We may never see a manger scene like this again—but we can remember. And when you're grown and far from home, keep this night in your little memory chest forever."

The years have passed and Ruthie is now a mother herself, living out in Phoenix. But never a winter passes she doesn't remember little Teddy, the picture window framed in colored lights, and the crowd of spectators standing in the December darkness, silent and awed as if in the presence of the First Christmas.

The Flying Trapeze

Easter in the Tinyburg Church isn't Easter until you've seen the annual Passion Play directed by Candice Spiller. Big crowds attend, including visitors from Bigtown thirty-five miles away.

Jimmie Swan, dishwasher at the Tinyburg Nursing Home, plays the role of Jesus. Because of his slender build, the stage hands easily lift him in place on the make-believe cross. As a stand-in, Candice uses her husky son-in-law, Jack Easley.

A year ago, the Reverend Doctor Henry Moss, pastor of the prestigious Bigtown Church, attended the Easter play. The attentive audience, squeezed into every available seat, impressed him. Alert for new ideas to draw people to his own church, he introduced himself to Candice: "Say, your play's a knockout. Better than what you see on Broadway. How about bringing your show to Bigtown next year?"

Candice was pained that Reverend Moss referred to her pageant as a "show." Yet she understood Reverend Moss, always thinking in grandiose terms.

Before she answered, Reverend Moss continued, "Naturally, we can improve the show. You need a bigger cross, elevated so everyone can see. Also, instead of those homemade wooden swords with blunt points, I'd go to a theatrical supply house and rent real ones with sharp edges, the kind that glisten under the stage lights.

"Another thing, I'd rig up a guy wire with a pulley and shoulder harness for the resurrection scene, so we can show Jesus rising in the air, lift him all the way to the ceiling."

"Never thought of that," offered Candice, her excitement growing.

"Now what you do here is OK for a small-town setting. It was a touching scene the way you directed Jesus to step up on a small riser, arms extended, his long, white robe rustling in the breeze from that oscillating fan you hid behind a tub of palms. But with our high ceiling and oversized stage in the Bigtown Church, we can elevate him clear to the ceiling in the resurrection scene. Slow and majestic-like, of course, because you don't want it to look like a trapeze act."

Candice wondered if she had the equipment for such a production.

"That's where I come in," boasted Reverend Moss, never one to underestimate himself. "Our church will provide everything —symphonic recorded music, bigger floodlights, authentic costumes from a theatrical supply house, whatever it takes. And we'll print oversize souvenir programs, run pictures of the cast in the Bigtown News. Just bring your show to Bigtown, and we'll pull out all the stops."

Again, Candice winced at the word "show." And she knew souvenir programs meant selling ads to local businesses, just like a big-top circus. She wasn't sure.

But she promised to discuss the possibility with her own pastor, who, as it turned out, also had doubts. Rehearsals in Bigtown would take more time, maybe compete with some of the Tinyburg Church activities. And didn't it smack of commercialism?

Reluctantly, Candice gave in. Next spring, the Tinyburg Passion Play would be staged in the oversized sanctuary of the Bigtown Church, including an authentic resurrection that would lift Jimmie Swan, in the role of Christ, all the way to the ceiling, if not to heaven!

"What if the wire breaks?" asked Jimmie.

"Son, that's the last thing you need to worry about," explained Reverend Moss. "This is big-time showbiz, not your little Tinyburg amateur hour. We're professionals."

Rehearsals began a full three months before Easter. The cast drove hundreds of miles back and forth for practicing and costume fittings, but the excitement of performing before a thousand people made it worthwhile. Burt "Lit'l Bit" Moore joked with Jimmie that if a talent scout from Hollywood saw him on stage, he might be forced to resign his dishwashing job and move to California.

But nagging doubts robbed Candice of her sleep. In Tinyburg, her dramas touched the congregation spiritually and emotionally. Would the circus-like atmosphere in the Bigtown Church overshadow the deeper truths of the Easter play? What if something went wrong while Jimmie, in the role of Christ, was being hoisted by a thin wire to the ceiling of the Bigtown Church?

William J. Cutrell, better known as "Uncle Billy Told-You-So," said that's exactly why he was staying home. "If I want to see a show, I'll watch television," he told Candice. "I know Jimmie and the other players mean well, but Reverend Moss has spoiled it with his hoopla and ballyhoo. When he asked the Tinyburg Cafe to buy an ad in his souvenir programs, I said enough's enough. Imagine, a picture of steaming hot cakes and syrup on the back of a church bulletin."

The evening of the performance, an overflow crowd filled the Bigtown Church. Car pools and chartered buses had brought much of Tinyburg's population for the event. Bigtown members complained that outsiders were taking the best seats.

It was a beautiful setting as the Tinyburg players recreated the closing days of Jesus' ministry. His betrayal, agony in Gethsemane, trial before Pilate, and finally His sufferings on the cross were told with reverence and sincerity. The hushed audience felt transported back in time and space to the first Passion Week in Jerusalem centuries ago.

After Jimmie Swan, in the role of Jesus, was secured to the cross, a burly soldier approached him with drawn sword, its brilliance reflected in the white glare of the spotlights. Although designed for realism, it was really a collapsible sword for use in plays and movies.

With a fiendish display of contempt, the soldier poised the sword between Jimmie's bare ribs and gave a short but determined stab.

To his surprise and chagrin, the sword failed to collapse, making a small but ugly gash in Jimmie's side.

"You stuck me! You stuck me!" cried the startled Jimmie as he looked down at a trickle of blood turning his loincloth a deep crimson.

The audience gasped, shocked by the appearance of real blood. "This has gone too far," the Tinyburg Preacher whispered to his wife Carol, certain now that Candice and her players had been manipulated by the publicity-hungry Reverend Moss.

Candice, backstage, quickly signaled to dim the spotlights while increasing the volume of the recorded music. She and other performers, knowing it was an accident and not in the script, gently lifted Jimmie down.

"I'm not hurt," he apologized. "Just a nick." But a couple of friends drove him to the emergency room while Candice assisted her son-in-law, Jack Easley, onto the cross. The lights came on and the play continued.

Those near the front could tell a substitute Jesus was on the cross, for Jack is at least sixty pounds heavier than Jimmie and four inches taller. Yet the transition was so smooth that many spectators never gave it a thought.

Fortunately, Jimmie's wound was superficial, requiring only four stitches and a precautionary antibiotic. He returned in time to watch the closing scene—Jesus ascending to heaven.

For the ascension, Candice played the "Hallelujah Chorus" at full volume, while an electrician switched on all the footlights, bathing the stage in a brilliant display of color. It was enough to move a confirmed agnostic.

But there was another problem. The stagehand who operated the pulley on the cross couldn't get it moving. Sensing the problem, three helpers rushed to his aid and with a mighty heave, started the heavier Jack on his slow ascent to the ceiling.

However, it wasn't what you'd call a slow ascent. With four men now putting their weight to the pulley, Jack literally shot upward on the wire, letting out a long, mournful, "Ohhhhhhhhhhh!" Then bang! His head struck the ceiling, momentarily dazing him. Instead of a victorious Christ, he looked like a limp scarecrow hanging on a clothesline.

Although Jimmie's wound a few minutes

earlier had been superficial, Jack's untimely ascent to "heaven" was real. A ripple of irreverent laughter spilled across the church.

Candice Spiller wished she'd never heard of Reverend Moss, the Bigtown Church, theatrical swords, or guy wires to heaven. If she could find a hole somewhere, she'd crawl inside and hide there the rest of her life. She now faced the embarrassment of another actor being whisked off to the hospital, a big lump on his head.

She consoled herself by promising never to direct a play for anybody, anywhere, anytime, including Tinyburg.

But the worst was not over. As the congregation filed out, she overheard someone whistling:

> Oh, he flies through the air
> With the greatest of ease,
> The daring young man on the flying
> trapeze....
>
> —Author Unknown

Yes, Reverend Moss was correct: Candice Spiller had brought her "show" to Bigtown! Driving home, she felt as if she were in a funeral procession en route to her own grave.

Uncle Billy "Told-You-So" gave little consolation, acting surprised the "show" turned out as well as it did.

Two people—whom she called angels—rescued Candice from her depression. The first was Jimmie Swan, who admitted that although the ordeal was humiliating, he gained a powerful insight. "I guess I'd looked at Bible stories as just that—stories from history which have little bearing on life. And Jesus, well, I idolized Him as a superman who never hurt or cried. But when that sword cut me—or maybe I should say pricked me—it hurt enough to tell me Jesus' suffering was real, too."

Then an unidentified caller telephoned from Bigtown. "I've been what you call a skeptic, saying the Bible is make-believe. You know, neat little stories with perfect endings. But something about the realism of your play revealed another side of the crucifixion story. Ours is an imperfect world where things never go exactly as planned. I liked the honesty and yes, the imperfections, of your pageant. It gave me a new perspective."

A couple of Sundays later, Uncle Billy asked Jimmie if his sore was healed over. Jimmie unbuttoned his shirt for him to run his fingers over the ridges left by the stitches.

"It's a real scar," Uncle Billy said. "Wasn't certain whether this was another stunt by Reverend Moss. Guess I'm like Thomas, the doubting Apostle, who said that except he put his finger into the print of the nails and his hand into Jesus' side, he wouldn't believe. Whatever it takes to bring out the truths of the Bible is maybe worth a little showmanship."

Which is why Candice continues to direct the Christmas and Easter pageants. But don't go to Bigtown to see her dramas. They play only in Tinyburg, where there are no guy wires to heaven. Only the stairsteps of faith!

The Jigsaw Puzzle

Although quiet and shy, Carl Bradley is one of Tinyburg's most tender-hearted citizens. An elderly man who lives alone, Carl operates a small business in his home. He's a woodcarver, turning out handmade toys and knicknacks which he sells to gift stores. He's also the faithful bellringer at the Tinyburg Church, rarely absent in spite of weather or illness.

A slight speech impediment adds to his shyness. "Don't ask me to talk in public, sing, or greet people," he told the Preacher when he joined the church. "My job's doing things with my hands."

He keeps the church nursery supplied with simple puzzles and handmade toys. Each puzzle consists of about six big pieces which small children can fit together.

When Eileen and Henry Becker moved next door to Carl, he welcomed them by giving a puzzle to each of their children. Bright kids, they quickly assembled the puzzles and begged for harder ones.

Carl apologized. "I'm sorry I don't have the equipment to cut those big 500-piece puzzles for older kids like you."

As they got better acquainted, Henry suggested Carl buy the kind of saws which make puzzles with as many as 500 pieces, which he did. Where possible, he chose scenes of local interest for the puzzles, which made them even more popular. His best seller was a puzzle of an aerial photo of the village of Tinyburg itself.

Each time Carl designed a new puzzle, he gave one to the Becker children, to see how they liked it, sort of test-marketing. The truth is, Carl never made a puzzle the Becker family didn't like. Putting the puzzles together grew into a family hobby. The kids raced against the parents to see who could finish first. This pleased Carl. "You kids could put my puzzles together blindfolded. Next you'll want a 1,000-piece puzzle!"

Whether it was Christmas, birthdays, or

anniversaries, the Beckers kept buying puzzles until the closets and shelves were running over.

"Hope I didn't start an epidemic," Carl joked to Henry.

"Not at all," replied Henry. "Solving puzzles is great for our family, something we enjoy doing together."

One Christmas the Beckers gave Carl a family portrait, in color. Carl was as proud as if it were his own family. Setting it on the dresser, he asked himself, *Whoever saw a handsomer couple and nicer-looking kids?*

There came a time, however, when the Becker family began to unravel. In real life, the happy faces in the family portrait started to fade. Living next door, Carl was one of the first to notice. Henry and Eileen yelled at each other at the slightest annoyance. It was as if they had kicked patience out the back door. Their hostility spilled over into the whole neighborhood. Carl saw it in the eyes of the youngsters—a hurt, questioning look, as if they knew something terrible was happening, but were too helpless to stop.

Carl, a man of few words, never dreamed of interfering. But one day while Henry watched him stamp out a new puzzle, Carl said, "I believe if you and Eileen worked as hard putting your marriage together as you do solving puzzles, you'd make a go of it."

Henry had a ready answer. "Carl, when you cut out a puzzle, you know those pieces will fit. You make them to fit, design them to work. Marriage *ought* to be like that. And if a fellow finds the right woman to begin with, problems will work out. But with me and Eileen, well, some of the pieces were missing from the start. I don't think our marriage was ever intended to succeed. I'm not made for her, she's not fitted for me."

Carl hesitated to say more, then added that raising a family is more complex than solving a puzzle. "I can determine the number and shape of a puzzle's pieces, guaranteeing anyone can put it together. But marriage never comes with a money-back guarantee. A couple can stage a wedding in a few minutes, but a marriage takes a lifetime."

"Carl, you've got your ideas, and I've got mine. And my idea is that the Becker family puzzle was never intended to be solved. Too many pieces are missing, and I don't have the patience to look for them. I figure it's easier for each of us to pull out."

"And what about the kids?"

"Don't worry about them. They're old enough to face reality. If Eileen and I split up before more damage's done, they'll be better off."

Carl let the conversation drop, worried that the Beckers were in worse trouble than he imagined.

Six months later the Beckers filed for no-fault divorce and put the house up for sale. As a family, they'd solved their last jigsaw puzzle. The morning they moved was heart wrenching. Assorted vans and pick-ups backed into the drive while Henry and Eileen sorted "his" and "hers." The atmosphere was icy, the children quiet and almost cowed.

Carl stayed at home, busy in his work-shop. Late afternoon, Henry brought Carl a $50 check, asked if he'd clean up the mess in the house, take anything he wanted that was left, and mow the lawn. Carl also promised to sort and forward their mail to separate ad-dresses, hugged Henry, and said he was sorry. Henry said nothing as he hurried back to one of the pick-ups and drove away.

While cleaning the house, Carl sifted through the closets for odds and ends left behind. Most of it he pitched in the trash: old magazines, a rusty can opener, a couple of puzzles with pieces missing, a spoiled jar of homemade pickles, a little girl's purse turned inside out, a pair of boy's faded swimming trunks, half a bag of cat litter, and two stale doughnuts from their last breakfast.

What broke his heart was a smashed picture thrown out in the backyard, as if on purpose. Inside the shattered glass was the Becker family portrait, identical to the one they had given him last Christmas.

He cleaned up the broken glass, removed the picture from the battered frame, and took it home. Now he had two prints of the family portrait he thought so much of. It grieved him to look at the happy faces and bright eyes of the children, knowing that in real life the smiles and happiness were gone. Could the Beckers ever be united? Or would the divorce be finalized, forever splintering them into pieces, like the shattered picture frame?

He slept poorly that night. Was it nightmares about jigsaw puzzles, stale doughnuts, and broken pictures?

When morning came, Carl Bradley was determined to cut out two more puzzles for the Beckers. He'd send one to Henry, one to Eileen, hoping they'd put them together.

Going to his workbench, he mounted both family photos on pressed wood, the one he'd picked up in the backyard, plus the one he got for Christmas. On the back of each puzzle he stenciled the following message in white letters:

> Love is **becoming** the right person, not just **finding** the right person.

Then he wrapped and mailed one to each of the Beckers's forwarding addresses.

Cynics who say the day of miracles is over will doubt what happened. But it did. When Henry, who had custody of the two boys, opened his puzzle, the three of them put it together in minutes. "Dad!" shouted the youngest, "it's you and Mom, and us kids! It's like our family's together again!"

Henry said nothing to reassure the boys his marriage would ever be better. Until, that is, he read the motto on the back, "Love is **becoming** the right person, not just **finding** the right person."

"What does that mean?" asked the oldest son.

"I guess it means you can solve most any puzzle if you become the right person," replied Henry, hesitantly, as if he wanted to believe it but was unsure.

A similar thing happened when Eileen and their daughter assembled the puzzle. Something magical took place as they, too, watched their family portrait slowly emerge from the jagged pieces of the puzzle.

After the reunion, the Beckers chose not to move back to Tinyburg. They decided to start over in a new community, free from old and poignant memories. Most of their old friends have forgotten them. But not Carl. He still remembers. Fact is, the Beckers won't let him forget. They're always calling, anxious to order his newest puzzles.

When the Beckers returned one of the family photo puzzles to Carl, he framed it, and you can see it on his dresser today. The Beckers also framed theirs, and whenever they look at it they remember that life is often a difficult, jagged puzzle, a puzzle that has more to do with becoming than finding.

Plywood From Heaven

In 1936, John Burke wrote the words to "Pennies from Heaven," a song that cheered millions during the Great Depression. Well, it's never rained pennies in Tinyburg, but one summer it did rain plywood. Or that's how it seemed.

For weeks, Carl Bradley had pestered the Tinyburg street department to repair a pothole in front of his house. "If it gets any bigger, someone's going to step off in it and never come up again."

His neighbor, Uncle Billy Cutrell, agreed: "You never saw holes that big when I worked for the street department. I took pride in my work. But it's different now. All some folks think about is their next paycheck."

"Sometimes I feel like fixing that hole myself," Carl replied. "Fill it with gravel and send the bill to the city."

Although Uncle Billy sympathized with Carl about the pothole, he gave him little sympathy about the "Going out of business" sign on his crafts shop. He told Carl to keep working, using himself as an example, being custodian of the Tinyburg Church.

Although he's nearly eighty, Carl's one of the busiest men in Tinyburg. "You've got one job, while I've got three," he reminded Uncle Billy. He rings the church bell, winds and sets the courthouse clock, and operates a small wood carving business from his home. He carves little crafts which he sells to gift shops, including jigsaw puzzles from plywood.

His favorite puzzles are the ones he makes for preschool children. They consist of only five or six big pieces, which youngsters assemble to make fish, ducks, lions, dogs, and ponies.

"I see no reason for a man my age to keep working," he told Uncle Billy. "Oh, I'll still ring the church bell and tinker around with the courthouse clock. But arthritis in my hands gives me pain. My home's paid for and I don't need the money, so why push myself?"

Dr. Gordon felt otherwise. Like Uncle

Billy, he advised Carl to keep working: "Keep those fingers flexible; once you stop, the arthritis will worsen."

Still, Carl figured he knew more about how he felt than Uncle Billy and Dr. Gordon combined. When his inventory of wood and paint was used up, he was quitting.

Meanwhile, a salesman at the Tinyburg Lumber Company had shown him a new grade of plywood for his puzzles. "Mr. Bradley, this is the finest, pre-finished plywood money can buy. Premium quality. We get it only on special order. How about me ordering you some, say a dozen sheets?"

But no, Carl's mind was made up; the shop was closing.

Carl was eating lunch on Tuesday when he heard a big clank-clunk, like a collision. Looking out, he saw a delivery truck limping down the street, having hit the pothole at a pretty good speed.

"It's a wonder he didn't blow a tire," Carl thought as he walked out to inspect the hole for the 132nd time. Then his eye caught a big sheet of plywood, which apparently bounced off the truck. As he dragged it into his yard, so no one would run over it, he noticed it was the same pre-finished plywood the lumber salesman had described.

Assuming it belonged to the local lumber company, he called to tell them, but they said no, their truck was sitting on the lot, and besides, they didn't have a single piece of premium plywood in stock. "Must be an out-of-town truck," the clerk said.

Carl propped it against a tree where it could be seen and fastened a homemade sign, "Lost." When Uncle Billy spotted the sign, he said it should read "Found." So Carl changed the sign to "Found." (When another neighbor questioned the word "Found," Carl made a third sign, "Lost *and* found"!)

Well, lost or found, no one claimed the plywood so Carl carried it into his shop to cut into puzzles.

Uncle Billy advised him. "Carl, finding that plywood is like the children of Israel eating manna from heaven in the wilderness."

"What's that to do with plywood?" asked Carl.

"You believe the Bible, don't you? You believe God saved the Israelites from starving, don't you?"

"Yes, I believe it happened to them a long time ago, but I don't see it happening in Tinyburg, if that's what you mean."

"What I mean," continued Uncle Billy, "is that your free plywood could be an omen from heaven. Here you were, ready to retire and stop making those pretty puzzles for the little kiddies. And you let your stock run low. So here drops a premium sheet of plywood, a sign you're to keep working."

"The only sign I see is that a truck nearly broke an axle because of our dilatory street department. Has nothing to do with manna from heaven, or that I'm to do anything I don't want to. Period!"

But Uncle Billy kept arguing. "I say manna's where you look for it, and if God allowed something usable to fall off a truck in front of my house, I'd make good use of it."

But Carl insisted. "I'm closing shop the first of September, manna or no manna, heaven or no heaven, signs or no signs."

That night Uncle Billy made a list of Carl's twelve best friends. Then he contacted each one, starting with Burt Moore. "Burt," he began, "if Carl Bradley died, would you give toward a memorial for his work as our bell-ringer? Maybe send flowers to his funeral."

"Sure—but I hadn't heard. When did Carl pass away?"

"I didn't say he died, I said *if* he died."

Burt looked relieved, but asked why Uncle Billy raised such a question when Carl was in good health.

Uncle Billy then repeated Carl's plan to close his shop, but how he needed to keep working, especially for his own good, and how this one sheet of plywood, a windfall from heaven, sort of marked the end of his career.

Then Uncle Billy made his pitch: "If you'd send flowers for his funeral, would you give the same amount while he's living? Enough to buy just one sheet of that premium plywood? Enough to keep him working another week?"

Within days, all twelve friends agreed to buy one sheet of plywood apiece.

Feeling like Santa Claus in the middle of summer, Uncle Billy arranged with the Tinyburg Lumber Company to deliver the plywood, but only one sheet at a time: "Deliver it about noon every Thursday, when he's uptown winding the clock. Lean it against the poplar tree in his front yard."

Carl was mystified. "Someone's playing tricks on me," he confided in Uncle Billy.

"You may call it a trick but I call it manna," Uncle Billy grinned. "Why worry where it comes from? The plywood's free—go ahead and cut it into puzzles."

Which he did, only in early August he dreamed that plywood was stacked in big piles around his house, so high he couldn't get out. The stacks reached a hundred feet or more, shutting off the summer breezes, while he gasped for air.

When he asked Uncle Billy what he thought the dream meant, Uncle Billy acted like Joseph before Pharaoh in the Old Testament. "Your dream's a symbol of how you've neglected your talents, closing your shop and disappointing your little customers. If you insist on retiring, you'll choke to death."

Carl said that was a little harsh on God's part to treat an old man that way, but admitted some truth in Uncle Billy's advice.

Anyway, about the third week in August, after the tenth delivery of plywood, Carl placed this ad in the *Tinyburg News*:

> To whom it may concern, Greetings. After reconsidering, I've decided to keep my shop open. Now taking early orders for Christmas. P.S. If our street department had half the gumption I do, they'd fix the pothole in front of my house.
>
> Carl Bradley

That fall was as busy as anytime in Carl's career. By Thanksgiving, he had more Christmas orders than he could fill. But there was a new rhythm in his work, a new joy in his heart. Customers who walked in unawares often heard him singing, "Every time it rains, it rains, plywood from heaven...."

Oh, yes. The Street Department fixed the pothole the same day he took down the "Closed" sign.

Jimmie Saves His Job

Jimmie Swan feared he was about to lose his second job as chairman of the happiness committee at the Tinyburg Nursing Home. His paid job is washing dishes, but he sort of appointed himself to the happiness committee. As he often says: "It's fun to joke with the patients, say a good word here and there. I can make anyone laugh. And since everyone here is over sixty, I never ask, 'How you doin', young fellow?' People want to be accepted for who they are, not what they once were."

To Jimmie, age twenty-eight, who's single, lives in a small apartment, and rides a bicycle to work, the residents are his extended family. If they're depressed, he's depressed. If he brings them joy, he feels good himself.

That's why he worried if he'd lost his magic touch when an eighty-six-year-old patient failed to respond to his humor. Her name is Lois, practically helpless, except her mind, which is exceptionally sharp.

Lois reared a large family, all of whom are now parents and grandparents themselves. No one needs her. And if anyone did, what could she do?

Now she was reduced to letting others do for her. Dressing her, bathing her, holding her unsteady arms while she took a few, faltering steps. This humiliated her and made her feel useless. Her only outlet was writing poetry.

She isn't a published poet, but she enjoys writing little verses about nature, babies, family, and God. Only now she couldn't hold a pen. If she composed a poem, she dictated it to a volunteer. "What's the use?" had become her byword.

Jimmie, whose bouncy enthusiasm makes anyone smile—at least for a minute—couldn't make a dent with Lois. She was crippled by the nightmare that not one person in the world needed her.

One morning when Jimmie stuck his head in her room to say hi, he found her in a deeper depression than usual. "Look at this!" she said, pointing to a bold headline in the morning paper:

Brother and Sister
Die in Home Fire

SCRANTON, PA—Billy Lewis, 5, and his sister, Anita, 3, died of smoke inhalation in their home here when a space heater exploded. Firemen, who tried desperately to reach them, said they probably were smothered to death in their sleep. The mother told police, "They're all we have. For years, we thought we'd never have children. Then Billy and Anita came like a gift from heaven. Why did God take them back so soon?"

"That's awful," whispered Jimmie.

"It's not only bad," replied Lois, "it's enough to make a thinking person lose all faith in God. Look at me. I've lived my life. If God is love, why didn't He take me instead of that precious brother and sister? Most folks ask, 'Why *me*, Lord?' But in my case, I wonder 'Why *not* me, Lord?'"

"Lois, we mustn't play God," Jimmie replied.

"Who's playing God? I'm talking about plain old common sense. And fairness. Here I am, no good to anyone, ready to go anytime, and God goes off to Scranton, Pennsylvania, and takes two little, innocent children. Doesn't He have better things to do?"

Jimmie wondered if we must blame everything on God.

"Who else is there to blame? Who else is in charge?" Lois asked. "The Lord gives, the Lord takes away. It's His world. Yes, I hold God accountable. If He's as powerful as the Bible claims, He could have stopped that fire."

Jimmie knew it was useless to argue with Lois. Besides, he felt inadequate to discuss deep, theological questions.

Just then the intercom interrupted: "Jimmie, please report to the kitchen."

"Oh, I've stayed too long," Jimmie said—then hurriedly, "Lois, you once told me how poetry is an outlet for putting your emotions on paper. Let's see you make up a new poem today, saying exactly what you think."

"If I wrote honestly what I think of God right now, the words would probably burn holes in the paper."

Yet all day, Lois thought about Jimmie's suggestion. Could she verbalize her doubts? If so, what good would it do? Whoever read it would probably be shocked, not helped.

She was still sifting Jimmie's advice when she went to bed that night. As she slept, her subconscious helped to sort out her feelings and arrange them into words.

The next morning she sent for Jimmie: "I've got the poem in mind but need someone to write it down."

"What poem?" asked Jimmie, who took a minute to catch on.

"The one about my bad thoughts toward God, and why He leaves me here in this nursing home with nothing to do."

Jimmie volunteered, and after he washed the dinner dishes and mopped the kitchen floor, he returned to her room with pen and paper. "Talk slowly," he told her, "so I can get every word."

Lois, seated in a wheelchair, her hair white and thin, with frail shoulders and skin so transparent you could see every vein, slowly recited her new poem:

Why Not Me, Lord?

I've lived a Christian life,
I've given you a son, daughter, and wife;
I'm ready to come on home—
Why Not Me, Lord?

How I miss the loves of my life
Nothing lightens the darkness at night;
I'm sick, I'm tired and bored,
Why Not Me, Lord?

Lord, it seems so unfair
With all the beautiful children up there
These old bones so battered and torn,
Why Not Me, Lord?

To take one's life by his own hand
In God's eyes a terrible sin;
But let me beg of you once more
Why Not Me, Lord?

Each sad and lonely day
As I read the obituary page,
A beautiful young child called home,
Why Not Me, Lord?

Lord, don't you need a helper with silver hair
To count your angels in the air?
Is that your knock on the door?
Why Not Me, Lord?

Lord, it seems so unfair
With all the beautiful children up there,
Don't you need a helper with silver hair
To count your angels in the air?
Why Not Me, Lord...?

> —Bob Payne
> Georgetown, IL
> (used by permission)

Jimmie said her words were real pretty,
then asked, "As you wrote this poem, did you

find an answer to your bitterness about God and the fire?"

"I wish I could say yes, but I didn't. Oh, I'm a big one for asking questions. It's the *answers* that bug me. But yes, Jimmie, I feel some better. Like you said, expressing your fears in words is like flushing an infection out of your system. But it still puzzles me why God leaves me to waste away to nothing, while He takes two precious children, young and vibrant. Probably no one can explain it. Maybe I'm asking too much."

As time passed, Jimmie detected a slow change in Lois. She smiled oftener, shed some of her self-pity as she resumed her habit of writing a few verses a day. Some of her verses were humorous, nonsensical, some serious. Invariably, her little poems touched on the deep mysteries of life, the questions we all struggle with.

A nurse's aide encouraged Lois to keep writing. "Your poems touch us. Everybody's struggling under some kind of burden."

One day a meat salesman called on the nursing home. While drinking coffee with Jimmie in the kitchen, he mentioned that his hobby was writing gospel music. Jimmie showed him Lois' poem, "Why Not Me, Lord?" and asked if he might set it to music. "It would please Lois," Jimmie added, "for she never thinks her work amounts to much."

The salesman read her poem and in minutes began to hum a tune to match the words. He took the poem with him, and in a few days mailed Lois a letter, enclosing a simple melody for her verse.

"Someone get Jimmie," she cried. "Tell Jimmie to come to my room right now, I don't care how busy he is washing dishes. Let the patients eat on paper plates!"

When Jimmie saw the music score, he praised Lois again. "You have a beautiful way with words, and now your new friend has given them a melody. I'm going to ask my friend, Candice Spiller, to come sing it for everyone to hear."

That night in the lounge, the patients gathered to hear "Why Not Me, Lord?" sung by Candice from the Tinyburg Church. Lois beamed; you'd have thought she had won an Academy Award.

"Are you happy now?" wondered Jimmie.

"Yes and no. I can never be happy like I once was. But I'm happier than I was yesterday." Then she asked Jimmie if he were happy.

"Can't you tell by the way I look? Now I can keep my job as chairman of the happiness committee. If I hadn't put a little sparkle in your eyes, I'd be fired by now!"

Lois continues to write poems at the nursing home. "Maybe that's why God doesn't take me," she often says. Then she adds, "It does a person good to put his feelings on paper, good or bad. I'll never learn all the answers here in Tinyburg. But then there wouldn't be anything left to do in heaven! So I'll keep asking the questions here, and in eternity I'll be finding the answers."

The Karman Ghia

Never were two men so different, yet such good friends.

Burt Moore, sixty-eight, is a prosperous securities salesman, a proud grandfather with expensive tastes. An ambitious fellow, he's always wanting a "little bit more" of this and that. He and Mrs. Moore live in a fine home on Main Street, where two late-model cars sit in the drive.

Jimmie, twenty-eight, single, who lives in a small apartment on Elm Street, rides a bicycle to his job as dishwasher at the Tinyburg Nursing Home. Some of Jimmie's critics say he doesn't have the grits in the middle of his plate, but I assure you he does.

Their common interest is cars. Although

Jimmie can't afford anything but a bicycle, his hobby is collecting model cars. He and Burt are always trading car magazines and going to car shows together.

Both men joined the Tinyburg Church about the same time. Burt, who transferred from a megachurch in Bigtown, sees himself as an organizational genius. His first proposal, which the members shrugged off, was a time-and-motion study of the Preacher and church secretary. Few of the members take to his big ideas, but everyone likes him in spite of his brash, know-it-all attitude.

Burt and Jimmie met at a new members' dinner. Both were seated at the head table. As usual, Jimmie was late. Thinking he wasn't coming, Burt (always looking for "a lit'l bit more") helped himself to Jimmie's cherry cobbler. When Jimmie finally arrived, the church ladies hurriedly opened a can of peaches for his dessert.

This didn't upset Jimmie. Being with his friends is what gives him pleasure, not whether he has homemade cobbler or canned peaches.

Jimmie, who didn't grow up in a church, had a lot to learn. For example, whenever the Preacher asked a rhetorical question, Jimmie thought he wanted an answer. One Sunday, preaching on the dearth of Bible knowledge, the Preacher wondered out loud just how many knew where to find the Ten Commandments. Pausing for dramatic effect, he was shocked when Jimmie spoke up, "Have you tried the Yellow Pages?"

One day Jimmie invited Burt to his apartment to see his hundreds of model cars, neatly arranged on three long shelves in his bedroom.

"I've always appreciated fine cars," Burt noted, fingering a model of a British Jaguar. "A car says something about the owner, especially if you're in sales like me. You can't impress the public, driving around in an old jalopy."

"Here's my favorite," interrupted Jimmie. "This 1975 Karman Ghia, a sports car made by Volkswagen. The poor man's sport car, they called it. Very popular with teenagers. I've had this model for more than 10 years—wouldn't part with it at any price."

Burt confided he'd wanted a sports car for years but feared he was too old."

"Tell you what," grinned Jimmie. "Buy you a 1975 Karman Ghia—I mean the real thing, not a model. Make you feel like you're sixteen years old! I saw one over at Import Motors in Bigtown. Sharp. Restored to mint condition."

Burt savored the prospect of being sixteen again, so he drove over to Bigtown and fell in love with the Karman Ghia. On first sight, he knew he'd buy it. However, Burt likes to bargain. If necessary, he'd make a dozen trips to Bigtown and burn his last gallon of gas to whittle on the asking price.

Certain he'd buy the Karman Ghia, he hired a carpenter to add a carport to their double garage.

"The carport's for your car," he told his wife. "I need your space for the Karman Ghia," adding it would make him feel sixteen again.

Mrs. Moore replied, "Why not go all the way and buy yourself a little red wagon and feel like you're four years old?" Burt didn't think that was funny.

While dickering over the price, the time came for the monthly potluck for senior adults at the Tinyburg Church. Mrs. Moore had baked a casserole and asked Burt to drive up to the door so she wouldn't get wet, since it had begun to rain.

Burt knew for sometime his transmission needed repairs, but he'd put it off until he knew exactly what he'd need to pay for the Karman Ghia. Anyway, when he backed out of the garage and tried to shift to drive, intending to pull up close to the house, it stuck in reverse.

Gunning the motor, he backed out into the street, intentionally hitting a chuckhole, hoping the impact might jar something loose in the transmission. It didn't.

Running inside, he told Mrs. Moore the problem, that she'd have to walk out to the curb.

"No, I'll drive my car," she insisted, "and you can call a tow truck for yours."

"I'm not paying someone to tow it to a garage," he argued, his face reddening. "There's no law says I can't drive it backwards to the church, then back it to the garage."

"Not with me in it," she replied, grabbing her keys and heading to the new carport, where her car had been moved to make space for the Karman Ghia.

Since you can't maneuver a car backwards as easily and quickly as you can forwards, Burt was late for the potluck. And he was annoyed by other motorists who gawked at him and blew their horns.

En route, he complimented himself on solving a parking problem at the church. The trustees were frustrated because no one paid attention to the "No parking" sign in the handicapped space. Burt had proposed a big sign showing Moses in a long white robe, holding the commandment, "Thou shalt not even think about parking here," with his finger pointed to violators. The sign worked! In fact, it almost frightened the handicapped away!

Having reached the church, Burt gingerly backed into the parking lot. But in his tiny rearview mirror he failed to see Moses. Instead, he knocked him flat on his back, his finger now pointed heavenward, warning the angels not to park there!

Then, without thinking, he backed his car right up against the rear wall of the church building, realizing too late he was hopelessly boxed in. Resigned to calling a tow truck, he determined not to let his bad luck interfere with the delicious food waiting inside.

After dinner, the program chairman apologized that the guest speaker had failed to show up, wondering if the Preacher could say a word. "Maybe about something you read this morning."

The Preacher was at a loss for words, then remembered a quotation from the Danish philosopher, Soren Kierkegaard: "We all know that life can only be understood backwards, but it must be lived in the future."

The Preacher went on, "Friends, don't waste your energy looking through the tiny rearview mirror of life. You may be senior adults, but don't lose yourself in nostalgia. Dare to look through the big windshield of today; live in the present; shift into drive, not reverse."

Burt was convinced that someone had told him about his car trouble. "It's not fair for a minister to capitalize on problems of his members for sermon illustrations," he mused.

But back to the Karman Ghia. Before he could close the deal, the Men's Club in the church launched a drive to buy a van for an overseas missionary, one equipped with Bibles, gospel tracts, medicines, blankets, and visual aids—something like a mission chapel on wheels.

Burt, ordinarily generous, but uncertain about the final price of the Karman Ghia, gave only a token amount.

His neighbor, Uncle Billy Cutrell, who helped count the donations, told Burt he'd be surprised how much Jimmie Swan gave.

"Jimmie doesn't have that kind of money," Burt replied. "Wonder if he sold some of his model cars—surely not the Karman Ghia?"

When Uncle Billy said he'd seen Jimmie go in a hobby shop with a big package under his arm, Burt knew his fear was true. He had sold his favorite model car to help buy the mission van!

The same night, Burt dreamed he won a free vacation. When he checked in at the luxury resort, the desk clerk noted the unusual way he signed his name, Burt "Lit'l Bit" Moore.

"Man, how lucky can you get! You've come to the right place, where we smother our guests with a little bit more of everything. Not because you need these luxuries, but because you want them. To start, how about a relaxing evening of television?"

He seated Burt in an oversize recliner in a huge room filled with every kind of TV imaginable—Zenith, Motorola, Sony, Magnavox, Panasonic, General Electric, Emerson, RCA, Toshiba, Mitsubishi, Quasar, Curtis-Mathes, Hitachi, Sanyo, Fisher, Philco, Sylvania, and Sharp.

They ranged from five-inch screens to wallsize. Every imaginable set ever assembled under one roof. Plus 155 channels, including ABC, CBN, CNN, CBS, weather, country music, sports, Disney, news, financial, gospel, MTV, plus movie channels galore. A non-stop, twenty-four-hour entertainment center.

Burt asked for a thirty-six-button universal remote and settled in to watch CBS on a twenty-five-inch color Zenith.

"Don't need a remote," advised the clerk. "Here, we turn on every set at one time, full volume, with enough screens to watch all 155 channels at the same time."

Burt complained he didn't need to watch that many.

Whereon he was reminded again that the luxuries offered here were not based on need, but on a "little bit more" of this and that.

By bedtime, Burt had a headache and wished television had never been invented.

Preparing for bed was another nightmare, because his oversized suite, more like a warehouse, was crammed with beds—cots, pallets, single beds, double beds, queen size, king size, hammocks, hospital beds, water beds, feather beds, ad infinitum. All night, an alarm clock rang every half hour, a signal to get up and change beds. How he longed for a full night's sleep in just one bed! By morning, his headache was worse.

This was the pattern of his entire free vacation—an excess of everything, a lifetime of vacations crammed into a single week.

Waking from his dream, or nightmare, he was so glad he could enjoy one TV program, eat one meal at a time, sleep all night in one bed, and drive one car. Which made him wonder if he really needed the Karman Ghia, or would the same money do more good, invested in the mission van?

As you may guess, Burt canceled his order for the sports car and gave a generous offering to pay for the van.

When Jimmie Swan asked when he was taking delivery of the Karman Ghia, he said he'd changed his mind. "But, Burt, you said you wanted to feel like a sixteen-year-old again!"

"I do, but I'd rather help some underprivileged youngster, who's maybe 14 or 16, to feel that he's somebody in God's sight."

The remark puzzled Jimmie, because he didn't know it was Burt's offering which had paid off the mission van.

That weekend, Jimmie showed up at Burt's house with a package the size of a shoe box, gift-wrapped with a colorful ribbon and bow.

"Why this?" inquired Burt, meeting him at the door. "It's not my birthday, not Christmas."

"Go ahead and open it," Jimmie insisted.

Carefully removing the colorful paper, Burt found inside the 1975 Karman Ghia model car, prized so highly by Jimmie. He was relieved Jimmie hadn't sold it, but puzzled why he was giving it away.

"It's for you," Jimmie smiled. "You're my friend; I want you to feel sixteen again. Here, hold it carefully in one hand and spin the wheels with the other. Close your eyes; imagine you're driving down Main Street, and see if you don't feel sixteen."

Burt did as Jimmie suggested, and with the magic of his imagination—for a few minutes he *was* a sixteen-year-old again.

I hope you'll visit Tinyburg sometime—just seven miles south of Pretense. Go by Burt's house on Main Street—easy to find, for it's the only house on that street with a double garage and a carport. Pay special attention to the carport, for parked inside is a little red wagon!

Knock on the door and introduce yourself. Ask Burt to let you hold the little 1975 Karman Ghia. Close your eyes, spin the wheels, and I guarantee you, too, will feel sixteen again!

Uncle Billy's Last Stand

There's one Labor Day Uncle Billy Cutrell will remember forever. It's the day he stood up for saving the Tinyburg Church. At the time, Uncle Billy thought it was his last stand.

The day began peacefully enough. Most members of the church left early for their annual picnic at Willow Creek State Park, thirty miles south of Tinyburg. It was the first picnic Uncle Billy had missed in twenty years. He could taste the open-pit barbecue cooked to perfection by Clay Barker. But with a touch of stomach flu, he decided to stay home and nibble on cottage cheese and dry toast.

He was sitting in his backyard, reading about Tinyburg's first fast-food restaurant. According to the paper, a wrecking crew would clear the site on Labor Day so the contractor could start turning dirt for the new restaurant on Tuesday morning. The crew chose a holiday, when there would be less traffic to slow down the dump trucks hauling away the debris.

Suddenly, Uncle Billy heard what sounded like a small army. He walked around the house and to his surprise a bulldozer, plus a front-ender and six dump trucks, were pulling up in front of the Tinyburg Church.

Curious, he crossed the street, meeting a giant of a fellow wearing a baseball cap which read "One Day Wrecking Service."

"I'm Hank," the burly fellow told Uncle Billy. "We have a permit to demolish this structure. Someone's puttin' in a fast-food restaurant."

"This is no structure—this is a church," bristled Uncle Billy. "And a good one. Took years of sacrifice."

"I know how you feel," replied Hank. "Seems a shame to wreck perfectly good buildings. But that's progress."

"Something funny's going on," Uncle Billy replied. "We never voted to sell our church to anyone for anything, especially a restaurant."

With that he reminisced how his parents moved to Tinyburg years ago, how he'd grown up here, found the Lord here, had his wife's funeral in this church. . . .

"Wait," interrupted Hank. "I've got my orders, and every minute we stand here arguing costs me money."

"I'm not arguing. There's nothing to argue about. You got your orders mixed up."

"I didn't get anything mixed up," replied Hank with a growing impatience. "Here, fellows, start in front. Knock down the steps and front door, then bulldoze right through the middle!"

A desperate feeling seized Uncle Billy. The village offices were closed for the holiday and most of the church members were thirty miles away at a picnic. It was his word against what appeared to be a valid demolition permit. There was no time for words, only action.

Although he's eighty, Uncle Billy crossed the street to his house like a teenager, unfastened a padlock and short length of chain from an old doghouse, returned to the church, and before the wrecking crew realized it, chained himself to the panic bars of the front double doors. Then he cried, "Okay, tear it down. Haul everything, me included, to the city dump—doors, windows, pews, Bibles, hymnbooks."

Hank was worried about his crew, earning

double time for a holiday, standing idle. His first thought was to tear the doors off the hinges and pile them at a safe distance under a tree, Uncle Billy and all. Instead, he went to the church office and called his supervisor in Bigtown: "Got a religious fanatic over here. Chained himself to the front door."

"I'm no fanatic!" screamed Uncle Billy, loud enough to be heard by the supervisor in Bigtown. "You're the fanatics, and I'm going to sue you for every truck and bulldozer you own."

"Be right over," the supervisor told Hank. "Sit tight. Sounds like a mental problem."

En route to Tinyburg, the supervisor decided that if the community knew a fanatic was blocking civic progress, his company might avoid embarrassment, maybe a lawsuit. So on his car phone he called radio TINY-FM, which promised to send a reporter.

In fact, the newsman beat the supervisor there. He quickly interviewed Uncle Billy, promising to air his comments on the 12 o'clock farm report. The supervisor was pleased. If the police had to remove Mr. Cutrell forcibly, the public would understand.

Meanwhile, at Willow Creek State Park, Clay Barker had called the picnickers from their ball game, saying the barbecue was ready.

"Wait 'till I hear the noon farm report," interrupted Ted Spiller, who works at the Country Grain Elevator. Others listening to Ted's transistor radio were shocked: "Friends, before the farm report, here's a late story. An elderly gentleman has chained himself to the door of the Tinyburg Church. Says his name is Cutrell, and that if his church is hauled to the dump, they'll have to take him."

"That's Uncle Billy, my neighbor," cried Sarah Biggs. "He's the only Cutrell in town. Has he lost his mind? No one's thought about junking the Tinyburg Church. He had a slight fever with his flu—maybe it shot up and he's out of his head."

"Shhh," warned clay. "Listen to what the man's saying."

What they heard was enough to dull their appetite for lunch as the Preacher and church officers piled into a couple of cars and sped back to Tinyburg. "Eat the barbecue while it's hot," the Preacher hollered, "Then bring the leftovers to the church."

All the while, Uncle Billy continued to debate with the wrecking crew. Hank hoped that if they let Mr. Cutrell have his say, he'd soon wear out and go home.

Uncle Billy used the time to good advantage. "You fellows go to Sunday School? Last week we studied about Jeremiah, an unpopular prophet. He warned his people to be patient, to submit temporarily to the rule of King Nebuchadnezzar. Jeremiah wore a yoke around his neck, a symbol he meant business. If Jeremiah wasn't too good to wear a yoke around his neck, I'm not too proud to wear a dog chain."

At this point the supervisor sent Hank to the police to swear out a warrant for Uncle Billy's arrest, adding, "It's for his own good. He's out of touch with reality, all this talk about Nebu-what's-his-name and dog chains."

Before Hank could return with the police, the Preacher's party drove up from the picnic.

"What's going on here?" demanded Clay Barker.

"That's the point," replied a truck driver. "Nothing. We've lost half a day's work over this Jeremiah stuff. Take a look—here's the demolition permit from your own village office."

Clay studied the official-looking yellow piece of paper, then broke out laughing. "Look, it says 840 South Division Street. Our church is 840 *North* Division. You fellows got the wrong address."

Hank, now back with the police, looked sheepishly at the permit. "You're right. I saw only the word Division Street, assuming no street in Tinyburg is long enough to be divided into north and south."

As other members straggled into town from the picnic, they stopped by the church to see what in the world was happening. Uncle Billy was an instant celebrity. After the interview aired on TINY-FM, he was photographed by a newspaper reporter from Bigtown. The Associated Press wired the photo nationwide with the caption, "Modern-day Jeremiah takes his stand—saves historic church."

Never had Uncle Billy felt so important. Fact is, he got to feeling so good that he asked if any barbecue was left from the picnic.

Not only barbecue but plenty of other goodies, too. Soon the members spread a second picnic on the church lawn with the wrecking crew as guests.

"Another half hour off the job won't bankrupt us," Hank said, accepting the invitation. "But I'm surprised you good folks don't kick us off your property, knowing the havoc we almost caused your church."

After the last barbecue sandwich was eaten, and Sarah Biggs had sliced the last fried apple pie, Uncle Billy reassured Hank not to worry about confusing north and south: "Just be sure you know the difference between right and wrong, between life and death. Make sure you're on the highway to heaven. Jesus said the way is narrow and only a few find it. That's why we built our church—to point the way. That's why I chained myself to the door. I wanted to take a stand—if necessary, my last stand."

And so ended the most talked-about Labor Day picnic in the history of Tinyburg. Oh, yes, the new fast-food restaurant has since opened and business is booming. If you decide to eat there, remember it's on *South* Division. Also stop at the church on North Division. They serve a hearty menu—including the Bread of Life.

The Face in the Window

Ever since his mother died more than thirty years ago, Uncle Billy Cutrell has wished a thousand times he had a photo to remember her by. But he doesn't. No baby picture, no school picture, no wedding photo, not even a snapshot. The only image is her memory in his mind, which each year dims with age. Then a strange series of events made him wonder if miracles still happen.

It all began when a committee to plan Mother's Day in the Tinyburg Church decided on a photo display. Opal Baggett, chairperson, came up with the idea of pictures instead of memorial flowers. "No flowers on Mother's Day?" complained Edith Barker. "That's like Christmas without poinsettias!"

Opal pointed out that families could still give memorial plants and baskets, but the center attraction would be photographs of mothers in the congregation, either deceased or living.

The exhibit attracted lots of attention. Some of the pictures were brownish and faded with years, while others were in fresh, bright colors. Here and there were a few old-fashioned tintypes.

"Why are those old people so stiff and serious?" inquired Rhonda Spiller, Edith's granddaughter. "They look like they've seen a ghost."

Edith explained. "Back then it was a novelty to pose for the camera. To allow time for exposure, you sat real still, never moving a hair. It's not like today, when high-speed cameras can even photograph moving objects."

Although the antique photos were rigid and artificial looking, they were the ones everyone talked about. Members oohed and ahhed, "I remember her" or "Who in the world's that?"

Opal Baggett, who thought up the idea, was pleased when Carl Bradley said it was like having his mother back again to see her likeness in the center of the exhibit. "She would have been proud," he said, wiping his eyes with the back of one hand.

No one gazed longer at the display than Uncle Billy Cutrell. After services on Mother's Day, he stood around for quite a while, scrutinizing each photo as if for the first time.

"Uncle Billy, I can't find your mother's picture," said Sarah Biggs.

"Don't have one," he replied.

"Not even *one*? Burn up in a fire or something?"

"No. Mother never had her picture made. Oh, there was a baby picture, but I always heard she tore it up when she got older."

"Uncle Billy, I can't believe this. I can't imagine any mother refusing to have a picture made, at least for her family."

That's when Uncle Billy decided to let her in on an old family secret. "Sit down," he began. "You'll have to delay your Sunday dinner. It's a long story.

"Mother was born with a birth defect in the middle of her forehead. Today, dermatologists could remove it. Back then, living way out in the country, you just endured such things.

"The best way I can describe it is to say it looked like a big, mashed strawberry. As a girl, she combed her hair down over her forehead, but could never hide it.

"You know how kids are, how they tease.

At school, they nicknamed her 'Strawberry Shortcake.' Terrible thing to do, but some children are thoughtless. I did my share, too. I remember one boy who was scared of dogs. We called him 'Bow-Wow.' We'd slip up behind him, bark like a dog, and watch him jump. Cruel, but we did it. And Mother's generation did the same."

The church janitor interrupted, saying it was time to turn off the lights. "Go on home," said Sarah. "Soon as Uncle Billy finishes, we'll lock up."

Uncle Billy continued, "As I was saying, Mother was sensitive about that strawberry birthmark. When she was about seven, so I've been told, she ripped her baby picture from its frame and tore it to pieces. No amount of coaxing ever persuaded her to pose for another photo.

"She was so surprised when Daddy proposed that she refused, saying no man could love a girl with an ugly birthmark.

"Daddy didn't say nothing. He just took her in his arms and kissed her passionately, not on the lips but on the birthmark. I wasn't there to see it, of course, but that's the way she told me.

"Another thing. Mother made Daddy promise never to embarrass her by making her pose for a camera. Daddy agreed, saying he wanted a real flesh-and-blood woman to love anyway, not a photograph. So they were married. They did everything proper—a church wedding, flowers, short honeymoon. But no photos!

"After we children came along, there were family and school pictures, but Mother was always missing. Daddy never ridiculed her timidity. So, Sarah, that's why Mother's picture is missing. There is none, nowhere."

When he finished, the two sat quietly. Then Sarah spoke, "Uncle Billy, that's the saddest but prettiest story. Especially the part about the marriage. It's a love story if I ever heard one. And you mustn't blame your mother for refusing to have her picture made. Someday, one may turn up in an old trunk of keepsakes."

Uncle Billy shook his head, since no photo ever existed to begin with.

"What about a miracle?" wondered Sarah.

"I believe in Bible miracles, but even the Lord couldn't create a likeness of Mother out of thin air."

Later that summer, Carl Bradley, against his better judgment, went to an auction. Carl avoids sales, for invariably he gets spellbound with the magic voice of the auctioneer, Clay

Barker, and buys absolute junk. Well, not always, for sometimes he picks up materials for his hobby of carving wooden toys and puzzles for children.

This particular auction was for antique cameras and old prints from the Pride Studio, which had gone out of business fifty years ago. When Mr. Pride died, the family boxed up lots of stuff and stored it away. Now a grandson had decided it was time to dispose of what he thought was junk.

In his day, Mr. Pride, an excellent photographer, did much of his work on speculation. He often attended church homecomings and family reunions whether invited or not. There he made group photos, later offering them for sale. A somewhat eccentric fellow, he often neglected to market his photos, so that at his death he owned a big inventory of unclaimed photographs.

His grandson, on advice of the auctioneer, sold everything by the box, rather than single items.

The bidding went well, for buyers knew some of the so-called junk had value as collectibles. Before he knew it, Carl made a successful bid for one of the largest cartons.

Lugging it home, he scolded himself: "I should never trust myself at Clay's auctions.

He could sell an accordian to a one-armed mannequin."

Opening the box, Carl found fifty large prints of the same photograph—another example of Mr. Pride's strange custom of making photos he never tried to sell. The prints were of a large group photo made years and years ago. It looked like a congregation posing in front of an old, frame church. Yes, there was the lettering at the bottom: Homecoming, Tinyburg Church.

Carl studied it carefully, looking for familiar faces. But he recognized no one. How funny the women looked in their long dresses and hair piled on top of their heads. And the tousled children, and the men with their strange, stiff collars, as if someone were strangling them.

Carl's first thought was to give the prints away. Then he had a better idea, one laced with mischievousness. He would mount one of the photos on thin plywood, then carefully cut it into tiny pieces. Without revealing what the completed puzzle looked like, he would take it to the next senior-adult potluck.

Making a 500-piece jigsaw puzzle by hand takes hours of careful work. Carl didn't mind— what fun when his church friends tried to put it together with no sample to go by! One way to get even with auctioneer Clay Barker—make him stay until the 500th piece was in place!

After the potluck dinner, folks began work on the puzzle. "Give us a hint of what it looks like," begged Uncle Billy.

"Okay, one clue: watch for three words in the lower left corner of the puzzle."

The group quickly assembled the corner which read, Homecoming: Tinyburg Church. It had to be years and years old, for no one was recognizable.

That is, not until the last pieces fell into place, whereupon Uncle Billy squealed, "Look! Look! See that boy, about five years old, sitting on the ground, sticking out his tongue and pinching the neck of the youngster next to him? That's me. That's Uncle Billy. I'd know it anywhere—I remember those new knickers. That photo is at least seventy-five years old!"

As the others studied the photo more carefully, they, too, picked out family faces, a grandparent here, a great-aunt there. But Uncle Billy was the only one who found himself.

Then someone pointed to a face in the window, a young woman who had stayed inside the church, apparently thinking the camera wouldn't see her. She wore a sunshiny smile, and you could tell she was fascinated by the picture-making outside.

Carl asked Uncle Billy if he had any idea who the mystery woman was. He didn't, because her image was not sharp, like those standing outside. Clay Barker, who lives nearby, offered to run home for a magnifying glass.

Eyeing the face carefully through the glass, Uncle Billy's voice broke in his throat before he could say anything. Then, "That's Mother! It has to be. Oh, it *is* her, my own darling, sweet mother with the strawberry mark on her face! She didn't intend to get in the picture, but she did. Oh, Carl, bless you for making this puzzle. Bless Clay Barker for persuading you to buy the box of antique photographs. It's a miracle. Sarah Biggs predicted a miracle for Mother's Day, but I didn't believe her."

Although pleased, Uncle Billy regretted that Carl, not knowing its value, had cut the precious photo into 500 pieces.

"How about forty-nine extra prints?" replied Carl. "That's how many are left. Mr. Pride apparently put them aside until everyone forgot about them."

Uncle Billy said it was all the Lord's doing. Otherwise, had the photos been circulated in her lifetime, his mother would have been mortified, because she never dreamed the camera would pick up her image.

If you visit Tinyburg, you'll see that photo in many homes, because Carl gave away the extra prints to all his friends.

Often, Uncle Billy holds his copy and looks into his mother's eyes, framed by the window. She's looking at her friends in the churchyard. She's looking at her children, her husband who kissed her scar. She's in the background, but she knows, she watches.

And Uncle Billy wonders if somehow, when all the mothers in the world go to that Great Beyond, if some way, somehow, they still look on the faces of those they love...even the little boy who made faces at the camera?

Berry-Pickin' Time

"Hello, Mr. Cutrell? This is Miss Kitty at the Tinyburg Library. If I came over, would you help us with an oral history project?"

"Come on," replied Uncle Billy, always anxious to talk about old times. "I've got oceans of memories, and they go way back. I grew up on a farm before we heard of tractors, telephones, and television. Horse-and-buggy days, we called them—country doctors, home-churned butter, and chicken fried in lard before we invented cholesterol!"

The next day, Miss Kitty sat in the porch swing with Uncle Billy, while a tape recorder purred nearby.

"History's more than knowing who was president in 1890," Miss Kitty explained. "It also includes little things, such as home-churned butter you mentioned on the phone.

"Now what I want you to do is pick out a favorite boyhood memory and tell it in your own words. Nothing fancy or earth shattering. Just a beautiful memory."

Uncle Billy thought a minute: "I could talk into that recorder thing all day, so stop me when you want. As a start, I'll tell about berry-pickin' time."

As the tape spun round and round, and Miss Kitty gently rocked the swing, here's what Uncle Billy said:

"There were four of us kids, me and my two younger brothers and our baby sister. Summer was our favorite time on the farm, especially berry-pickin'.

"About the middle of July, Mother and Daddy set aside two days to pick and can blackberries. The first day we washed about seventy-five glass fruit jars, Mason jars we called them, plus the zinc lids and sealing rubbers. We built a fire in the backyard under two tubs of water, setting on bricks. Us boys carried the jars from the smokehouse, all dusty and cobwebby. We first sloshed them around in the tub of hot soapy water, then scalded them in the second tub of boiling water. Then we set the jars in the sun to dry.

"We also dragged the horse trough from the barn lot into the yard and filled it with cistern water. It was a big trough, much like an oversized bathtub. Daddy always made pets out of our cows. In August when the pond in the pasture dried up or was covered with green scum, we pumped the cows' drinking water into that trough from a deep well.

"Berry-pickin' was the only time we took a bath in the big horse trough. It was a treat, because we came home sweaty and itching from chiggers.

"Finally, Daddy drove the wagon into the pond, so the wooden wheels would soak up the water, swelling them to fit the metal rims.

"So with the jars sterilized and the trough filled for our baths, we were ready for berry-pickin' the next day."

"Uncle Billy, you make me wish I lived back then," interrupted Miss Kitty.

"Don't think it was all play. You can't imagine how early we got up. Daddy was a strong believer in milking cows before daylight. Why, I don't know. Some of our neighbors milked after sun-up, but not Daddy. He was always at the barn by four o'clock.

"Soon Mother was calling us: 'Berry-pickin' day!' as she pulled back the covers. 'Rise and shine!' After breakfast, we dressed for the berry patch. All you could see was our fingers and faces. We were dressed for war!

"To protect our arms from the sharp briars, Mother cut the feet out of long stockings which she pulled over our arms, snug to our shoulders. Then we put on bib overalls and long-sleeved denim shirts. She tied binding string around our pants and shirts at our ankles and wrists to keep out the chiggers. Then red bandanas around our necks. Only first she dipped them in coal oil—kerosene—and wiped our faces and ears. Coal oil was supposed to scare off the chiggers. Wide-brimmed straw hats shielded us from the July sun.

"Daddy, dressed the same way, hitched the mules, Rhody and Jack, to the wagon, filled the wagon bed with straw, and drove up to the back door. Mother spread a quilt over the straw while us boys loaded the supplies: baskets lined with newspapers to hold the berries, plus assorted buckets, pots, and pans. Mother climbed in with the baby, the lunch basket at her feet. At last we were off for the short drive to the back of our farm, near the old orchard. We knew the best berries were hiding back there, along the fence rows and the right-of-way of an abandoned railroad that skirted our farm.

"Oh, yes, I forgot Gray Boy."

"Was Gray Boy a neighbor?" asked Miss Kitty as she put a new tape in the recorder.

"Gray Boy was our hunting dog—begged to go everywhere. When he looked at us with those big, gray eyes, you could imagine they were filled with tears, pleading to go. 'Come on, Gray Boy, hop in!' Daddy said. Wagging his tail hard enough to shake the ground, Gray Boy bounded into the wagon. Standing up front, his nose pointed in the wind, you'd have thought he owned the whole farm—cows, mules, fences and all.

"We went through four gates before we reached the back of the orchard. Me and my brothers took turns opening the gates, Gray Boy barking orders as if he owned the fences. It was still early when we reached the back of the orchard. Lots of dew, but Daddy said it was better to get our pant legs wet than to sit around until the hot sun dried the grass. Daddy unhitched the mules to graze, while Mother spread a quilt under a tree where she could watch the baby and pick from some of the nearest vines.

"Daddy was the fastest berry picker ever. He picked with a two-gallon bucket, while we boys made do with half-gallon syrup buckets. You talk about berries. Berries, berries everywhere! We watched while Gray Boy wiggled through the bushes, hoping to scare some garter snakes that love to feast on berries. Overhead, blue jays scolded us for invading their berry preserve, although heaven knows there was plenty for everyone. We also battled yellow jackets, june bugs, honeybees, and flying gnats, while Gray Boy majored in rabbits, flushing out one after another.

"Fill your buckets and get back to the wagon to dump the berries in the baskets! Then again. And again. Miss Kitty, I close my eyes and see it all—butterflies skimming around the black-eyed Susans, Gray Boy chasing rabbits, a covey of frightened quail, baby sister crawling on the pallet, us boys dressed in our funny stockings and red kerchiefs, the smell of coal oil blending with honeysuckle.

"By eleven o'clock, we had picked enough berries to smother an elephant, the luscious, black fruit shining in the baskets.

"'Enough,' called Mother. 'More than I can ever work up. Wash your hands in the creek for dinner.'

"Off came the red bandanas, the binder string from our wrists, and the long stockings on our arms.

"Lunch was simple but hearty. We were so hungry, shoe leather would have tasted like roast beef. Mother fed us fried egg sandwiches, using leftover biscuits from breakfast. Daddy— believe it or not—had his own special sand- wich, made of thick slices of white, raw onions and mustard. I still see him, munching on that biscuit-onion sandwich. For dessert, Mother cut a chocolate layer cake, which we downed with big glasses of fresh lemonade, kept cool all morning in a gallon jug in a nearby creek.

"By noon, we were ready to hitch the mules and go home, our wagon bed groaning with mounded pails of berries. Four more gates to open and close, another chance for Gray Boy to stand in the front of the wagon like an Indian scout, then to bark excitedly as we pulled into the yard.

"You might think our work was over, but it was only beginning, especially for Mother. My brothers and I carried in firewood for the kitchen cook stove. We also drew gallons and gallons of clear water from the cistern to wash the berries of dust, insects, and bits of leaves. Now the berries were ready for cooking. My, how hot the kitchen got, with all that stirring and boiling and steaming. Finally, Mother poured the berries through a funnel into the sterilized jars, topping them with rubber seals and zinc lids. I remember how pretty the cans of berries looked as we set them on the back porch to cool. Their deep, red color reminded me of winter sunsets, of berry cobblers on cold nights, of blackberry jelly on homemade biscuits, of bowls of berries swimming in real cream.

"After dark, me and my brothers un-dressed in the back yard and hopped in the horse trough. We ducked each other and had water fights, while the soapy water, warmed from a day in the July sun, washed away the sweat and grime and itching of the berry patch. Then Mother and baby sister had a turn. Finally, Daddy took his bath, then dumped the water on Mother's rose bushes. She be-lieved soapy water made bigger blossoms.

"Tucked into bed, I relived the day, while Gray Boy snoozed on the front porch, dream-ing of rabbits as big as greyhounds. I fanta-sized of autumn, the first hard frost when Mother would open a jar of blackberries to make a cobbler in a deep baking dish, criss-crossed with pie dough. Coming home from school, I would smell the sweet aroma, peek at the bubbling juices as some spilled over into the bottom of the oven, creating a scorched but sweet aroma.

"Before falling asleep, I could hear Mother say to Daddy, 'For good measure, give the lids one more twist.' She always said this when she canned anything, knowing Daddy's strong farm hands could give the lids that final twist which made sure they sealed.

"Yes, Miss Kitty, those nine words, 'For good measure, give the lids one more twist,' stood for security...and family together-ness...and mouth-watering food...and all the good things that bless our lives.

"And you may find this hard to believe, Miss Kitty, but sometime when I'm sitting in church I see my Daddy's hands again, not just sealing lids on blackberries but doing all the good things fathers are known for."

"What triggers those memories?" asked Miss Kitty, wondering aloud if she should put another tape in the recorder.

"I think there's enough tape left, for I'm about finished. But what often revives that memory is a certain hymn, a favorite with our choir, about the hands of Jesus. Most folks think of it as a funeral song. But to me, as I remember Daddy's strong arms and hands, it becomes a hymn of life and joy:

> Safe in the arms of Jesus,
> Safe on His gentle breast,
> There by his love o'er-shaded,
> Sweetly my soul shall rest.
> Hark! 'tis the voice of angels,
> Borne in a song to me,

Over the fields of glory,
Over the jasper sea. . . .

Safe in the arms of Jesus,
Safe on His gentle breast,
There by His love o'er-shaded,
Sweetly my soul shall rest.

—Fanny J. Crosby

As Miss Kitty turned off the tape recorder, she thanked Uncle Billy for sharing a beautiful story, a memory that might never get into history books, but can never be erased from our minds.

A Mail-Order Baptism

"Guess who came in this morning, looking for an old farmhouse?" Clay Barker asked his wife Edith as they sat down for dinner.

Clay, president of the Tinyburg Realty Company, didn't wait for Edith to guess: "Marie Ralston—used to be Marie Berry. Grew up here, but's lived for years on a ranch out in Montana."

"Why's she coming back to Tinyburg?" Edith inquired.

"Her husband died, and she wants a smaller house with some acreage. So I'm showing her the old Blackburn place."

"Who'd want that ramshackle house? If a sparrow landed on it, the roof would collapse."

"I know," agreed Clay. "But she wants

something cheap—or underpriced as she calls it—that she can fix up herself."

"Good luck to her, but I wouldn't buy it for a doghouse."

That afternoon, Clay drove Marie five miles out the blacktop, then off on a gravel lane across a rickety, one-way wooden bridge to the Blackburn place.

It wasn't a pretty sight. A half-grown pup owned by the last tenant, looking as if he'd lost his last friend, was stretched out on the front porch. One of the wooden steps had rotted out, the gutters were rusty, the wallpaper in two rooms was peeling off, and a leaky kitchen faucet looked as if it had never seen a plumber.

But Marie said, "Just what I want. You can look in any direction and not see another house. I like privacy. You see, Clay, Mr. Ralston and I lived for years on a ranch with no close neighbors. We got used to it. Gave us a chance to live our own lives."

Although Clay wanted to make the sale, he felt he should caution her about repairs.

"No problem," she replied. "I'm what you'd call a do-it-yourselfer. Had to be out West. I can do anything a man can—carpentry, plumbing, you name it."

So to Clay's delight, the owners accepted

Marie's offer, and the next morning the parties were in his office to sign a contract.

"Sure surprised me," Clay confided to his wife. "Never dreamed a widow would choose to live way out there."

"Not me," replied Edith. "Aunt Sarah Biggs, who's known Marie all her life, told me how strange she acted, even as a kid. Withdrawn and aloof, that is. Understand she found her husband through a magazine ad.

"Aunt Sarah used to send her birthday and Christmas cards, but got no response. When Aunt Sarah vacationed in the West, she wrote Marie, thinking she might spend a night at their ranch. But she got no answer. Hopefully, Marie will be different after she moves back."

But Marie wasn't different "after she moved back." When church visitors called, she'd barely open the door, then hook the screen. "No, thank you," she said. "I'm not interested in church. Too much stand up and sit down and bow your head and shake hands with the visitors. I enjoy plain living. Sundays in the summer, I feel as close to God picking wild daisies as you do listening to a sermon. Maybe closer."

When Aunt Sarah visited Marie, she never mentioned church. "I understand Marie," she explained, "and if she makes up her mind to come, she will. In the meantime, she's on my 'hard cases' prayer list."

God apparently listened to Aunt Sarah's prayers, for within months Marie began to change. Would you believe God used some August peaches, a February ice storm, and an August baptizing to bring about the change in her life?

Back of the rundown house that Marie had bought are two old, gnarled peach trees. The first August she was there, she decided not to use a ladder, but picked what fruit she could, standing on the ground. "I've seen the time I didn't need a ladder of any kind—just shinny up the tree," she told Aunt Sarah. "But this year, I figured it's not worth the risk."

Aunt Sarah suggested, "Our Preacher's wife cans a lot of fruit. He'd probably pick them for you on shares."

So on the last Friday afternoon in August, the Preacher drove five miles out the black-top, crossed the one-way bridge, and pulled up in Marie's front yard. Long before sundown he had picked four bushels from the tops of the peach trees—two for himself, and two for Marie. He could have picked more, but a lazy thunderstorm in the northwest suddenly picked up speed.

He barely loaded his two baskets in the car when the rain started with a big whoosh. It was a cloudburst, the water rushing down the gullies on either side of the gravel road. His windshield wipers labored under the drench-ing rain as he kept a lookout for the one-way bridge. Fortunately, he slowed down before he reached the bridge, for the heavy rain had washed it out. Odds and ends of planks were floating down the creek, like old battleships going to war.

Since there was no other access to the main road, he walked back to Marie's. "I need to call Carol," he hollered through the screen door, above the sharp cracks of thunder.

"I'll call," Marie replied, hooking the screen door. On second thought, with unusual neighborliness, she unlooked the screen and invited him in.

"You're drenched! Here, use this bath towel to dry off. Then you can call Carol."

"Yes," Carol answered. "If you can wade across, I'll meet you this side of the creek. But what about the peaches?"

"I can wade across," the Preacher re-plied. "But no way I can carry the peaches, too. I'll give them to Marie."

Marie, grateful for the extra peaches, in-vited the Preacher to sit down and wait until the storm passed. "Sorry I hooked the screen door when you knocked," she apologized. "Bad habit, I know. My husband scolded me for always locking doors."

Since the storm brought on an early dark, Marie turned on a reading lamp. Its soft light flooded an attractive certificate, framed like a high school diploma. "Get that when you graduated?" asked the Preacher.

"Oh," laughed Marie. "That's a baptismal certificate. My husband's."

"I didn't think you were church people."

"Oh, we're not. Definitely not. Too many people use religion as a crutch. I'm a do-it-yourselfer. My husband was, too. On the ranch, we learned to look out for ourselves. Years of work and sweat. If more church people rolled up their sleeves and worked on Sundays, rather than down praying to God for this or that, we'd be better off. Get rid of welfare rolls, too."

"Then why the baptismal certificate?"

"Read it for yourself," she said, taking it down from the wall.

He read aloud, half to himself: "This is to certify that Mr. C. A. Ralston, upon his profession of faith in goodness, did on this day baptize himself in the name of truth, beauty, and love. Valid for membership in any church that will accept it."

Pausing a minute, the Preacher continued, "Mrs. Ralston, I never saw anything like this in my life!"

"Me neither," she smiled. "But near the end of his life, Mr. Ralston got to thinking about the hereafter. Answered an ad for this mail-order certificate. And only $5, postpaid. Cleverest little set of instructions came with it."

"He actually baptized himself?"

"Yes, I saw him! For sprinkling, you fill a cup of water, lean your head back like you was taking a big dose of bad-tasting medicine, and pour a few drops on your forehead. Then you say, 'I baptize myself in the name of truth, beauty, and love.'"

"And how about immersion?"

"That's what Mr. Ralston preferred, since we were raised that way. So one morning we filled a big watering trough, closed the gate to keep out the cattle, and let the hot sun warm the water. About sundown, he climbed in the trough, clothes and all, held his nose and ducked under. I brought him some dry clothes and he changed right there in the feed lot, and that was that."

"Was he sincere?"

"As sincere as he knew. As I said, both of us grew up independent. We don't depend on nobody for nothing, and that includes God, religion, or whatever you call it."

As soon as the Preacher forded the creek and climbed in the car with Carol, he retold the unbelievable story of the mail-order baptism.

Summer turned to fall and the following February, during an ice storm, a second bout with nature helped to soften the heart of the self-sufficient Marie Ralston.

It started when she slipped on the ice, breaking two small bones in her right elbow and bruising her left arm. As Dr. Gordon fitted Marie with a heavy, rigid cast from the wrist to the shoulder, he reminded her she couldn't stay alone.

"I bought me a house in the country, and I mean to make it my home, arm or no arm," she snapped. "I'm no invalid. My pantry's bulging with canned food and there's enough split logs on my back porch to keep my wood stove going all winter."

"I don't care if you live next door to a sawmill and a food cannery, you need help."

"We'll see," Marie said determinedly.

The following day, Aunt Sarah and the Preacher's wife Carol called on Marie. It was a pathetic scene—a half-opened jar of green beans which Marie had given up on, the fire almost smothered with wood ashes she couldn't carry out. Without a word, both women set to work—bringing in wood, washing dishes, preparing food, and shampooing Marie's hair with soft water from snow they melted on the stove.

For once, Marie was quiet and appreciative.

For ten days, some lady from the church did her housework. Then every other day. Then once a week, until spring melted the ice and restored feeling to her arms.

The do-it-yourself ranch woman from the West was beginning to find in her Tinyburg friends the closeness she had been running from. Not that Sunday found Marie on the front pew of the Tinyburg Church. Habits change slowly. Marie was wedded to her old traditions.

Then the dam broke, freeing Marie from her spiritual and emotional isolation.

It happened during Old Settlers' Week—an annual, community homecoming. The festivities end on Sunday, when the churches unite for an interdenominational service in the park.

This year, someone suggested the reenactment of an old-time, outdoor baptizing in the Gaynor Pond east of town. In the years before indoor baptistries, the churches baptized all their converts there. Since the younger residents had never seen an outdoor baptizing, the idea of a reenactment generated lots of excitement.

The ministers in Tinyburg drew lots to see who would do the baptizing, while George Mason, the barber at The Purple Crackerbox, volunteered to be the convert.

When Uncle Billy Cuttrell stopped in for a trim, he kidded George. "Think this will make you twice as good?"

"Uncle Billy, this town doesn't need more goodness," George shot back. "You've got enough goodness tucked away in your soul to out-goodness all of Tinyburg!"

On a bright Sunday afternoon it looked like the whole town gathered at the Gaynor Pond to hear a combined choir and witness an old-time baptizing. The children were fascinated, asking if Mr. Wilson would wear a life jacket, and what if he and the minister drowned? Even Marie Ralston was there, although she stood timidly toward the back.

The Tinyburg Preacher, who had been chosen to baptize Mr. Mason, spoke briefly:

"Jesus set us an example, being baptized

during an outdoor revival led by John the Baptist near the Jordan River. You see, John wasn't what you'd call a professional evangelist. He chose the streets and marketplaces for his pulpit, not the sacred hush of the temple. To Jesus, baptism was one way to identify with common people like John the Baptist. And today, when we're baptized, it's a symbol of our need for each other, to join hands with the family of God."

Then the choir sang so beautifully they almost embarrassed the angels:

> Shall we gather at the river,
> Where bright angel feet have trod?
> With its crystal tide forever
> Flowing by the throne of God?

—Robert Lowry

George Mason, led by the Preacher, now stepped into the water. A quiet hush fell on the crowd when suddenly, a woman's voice cried out. "Wait! If it's not too late, make this a *real* baptism—not a reenactment. George's been baptized once. He doesn't need it. Let me take his place."

A chorus of "Amens" greeted Marie as she made her way to the edge of the pond. "I may not be dressed in a white robe," she said, "but my faith's in the Lord and His people. I want to be part of God's family. For seventy-seven years, I've gone it alone. Self-sufficient was my middle name, but since returning to Tinyburg, you good folks have shown me how much we need each other. And we badly need the Lord. No one can save but Him. And it's impossible to properly baptize oneself, although my late husband tried. Today, I'm in the fold. I want to be buried and risen with my Lord!"

And as the Preacher gently lowered Marie into the water "in the name of the Father, the Son, and the Holy Ghost," the onlookers praised "God from whom all blessings flow."

Angel in the Night

Compared to Sarah Biggs, most folks in Tinyburg are Bible ignoramuses. She knows the Bible forward and backward, crosswise and lengthwise. If someone gave her a Bible printed upside down, she could probably read it! The Preacher calls her his "walking concordance."

However, Aunt Sarah's friends were skeptical of her offer to teach Bible lessons on radio TINY-FM. But Aunt Sarah argued that her lessons would be different. "I'll deal with topics you never hear on radio."

"Like what?" wondered Edith Barker.

"Like animals, that's what. Did you know the Bible mentions more than forty animals, including apes, donkeys, horses, bears, oxen, camels, deer, goats, lions, sheep, hogs, wolves, and weasels? Plus all kinds of insects, birds, fish, and reptiles, such as the serpent which tempted Adam and Eve."

When she approached the station manager, he, too, was skeptical. "Sounds more like a visit to the zoo," he replied, hoping not to offend her. "Besides, the air time allotted for religion is taken."

When Aunt Sarah insisted her Bible lessons were one-of-a-kind, he found a spot for her one night a week at three a.m.

"You mean three o'clock in the morning? Who in the world would listen?"

"You'd be surprised—people who work at night, truck drivers, insomniacs...."

"I was hoping for a better time slot," Aunt Sarah interrupted. "But beggars aren't choosers. Although three a.m. isn't the best time for a radio Bible study, I have many loyal friends who will set their alarms and listen." She then wrote this notice for the Sunday bulletin:

> Miss Sarah Biggs, teacher of the ladies class, can be heard at three a.m. Thursday on TINY-FM. Miss Biggs, who invites her many friends to listen, will teach a series on the animals of the Bible. Set your alarm so you can hear her very first program.

Sarah paid little attention to Uncle Billy Cutrell, who jokingly said she should apply for a job at the high school teaching zoology. "If you read the Bible more and the sports pages less, you'd appreciate the role of wildlife in the Scriptures," she replied.

Aunt Sarah was pleased when the program director taped her lessons, to save coming to the station in the middle of the night. The first time her program aired, she never went to bed, fearful she wouldn't wake up at three o'clock to hear herself. She wondered how big an audience would listen to her first program: "Thousands? Hundreds? How about fifty? Yes, fifty would be a good start. As word spreads, hundreds, even thousands, will be listening!"

On her first broadcast, Aunt Sarah read these verses from Job in the New English Bible:

> Consider the chief of the beasts, the crocodile, who devours cattle as if they were grass: what strength is in his loins! What power in the muscles of his belly! His tail is as rigid as a cedar, the sinews of his flanks are closely knit... for he takes the cattle of the hills for his prey and in his jaws he crunches all wild beasts.

Then she elaborated: "Radio friends, whether you call him a crocodile or behemoth, God made him, as he did all the animals of the plains and jungles, all the insects of the forest, all the fish of the sea. God is the source of all life. Even the animal kingdom is subject unto him."

With this, she told her audience good-night, hoping they'd listen again next Thursday morning at three a.m.

Sunday morning, she asked her class for a show of hands by those who listened to her on the radio Thursday morning. When no one raised a hand, she thought the ladies misunderstood, so she repeated the question. Still no response. She was crushed—not a single member had bothered to set her alarm to listen. And after all she'd done for this class— preparing lessons, mailing birthday cards, visiting them in the hospital.

So she just stood there, her bottom lip quivering, tears forming in her eyes. Then Edith Barker spoke up:

"It's not that we don't care. But three o'clock in the morning is asking a lot. If I got up that early, I might as well stay up the rest of the night, because I couldn't go back to sleep. Nothing personal, Sarah. But your program is at such an odd time and also, a Bible study on animals isn't all that exciting."

Since Aunt Sarah doesn't quit easily, she

put the same notice in the bulletin, week after week: "Miss Biggs invites her many friends to listen to her program at three a.m. Thursday morning on the animals of the Bible. Set your alarm and tune to TINY-FM."

And each Sunday she asked for a show of hands by those who listened. Occasionally a hand went up, but never more than two. Another disappointment: no fan mail, not even a post card. But she encouraged herself with the fact she was learning much about wildlife in the Bible, even if no one listened.

On the tenth broadcast she lectured on sheep of the Bible, how in Old Testament times before coinage was invented, riches were measured in the size of one's flocks. She told how Abraham and Lot argued over water rights and pasture for their livestock.

She described how sheep were domesticated as early as 3,000 B.C., long before the camel. She listed the three species in Palestine: the short-tailed horned sheep, the broad-tailed sheep, and the long-legged Egyptian-bred sheep. She told the five uses of sheep in Bible times: food (milk, cheese, meat); clothing; oil and unguent flasks made from horns; tent coverings; and offerings to God.

Aunt Sarah pictured the helplessness of sheep, their dependence on the shepherd whose voice they knew. She described the festive sheepshearing after the spring lambing season, a time of feasting and family get-togethers.

She closed by reading Psalm 23, emphasizing that "the Bible says the Lord is *my* shepherd, not merely *a* shepherd." She paid tribute to Jesus the Good Shepherd who lays down His life for His sheep.

After taping the sheep program, she questioned again if it was worthwhile. "All this study and nobody listening."

When she arrived at the studios the following week to tape another lesson, the receptionist handed her this letter, the first fan mail in ten weeks:

To whom it may concern: Last Thursday I picked up your station about three o'clock in the morning. I didn't get her name, but it was a woman talking about animals of the Bible. I had been driving all night, going home for the funeral of my aged father. Although I'm a Christian, I didn't want to hear any preaching. I guess I was angry at God, angry for letting my Dad suffer so long and angry that death robs us of those we love the most.

Dad was a farmer who also raised a few sheep. He made pets of them, gave each a name. Nearly killed him to sell any. As a boy, I was given one to care for. Dad told me,

"Sheep are helpless in face of danger; be good to them."

Then this lady, whoever she was, read Psalm 23. It brought back memories of how tenderly Dad cared for our small flock. And I was reminded that Dad is now in the care of the Good Shepherd of heaven. Suddenly, my resentment toward God melted away. Blinded by tears, I pulled off on the right-of-way. There I let all my sorrow spill out and when I finished crying, I felt an inner peace you can't describe.

So I want to thank the lady who was on the radio at three o'clock in the morning. She touched my heart. Please give her this note. To me, she was an angel in the night.

(Signed) Cecil Hauser

Now it was Aunt Sarah's turn to cry. Overcome with emotion, she asked to come back tomorrow to tape her program. "I'm in no condition to say anything now," she told the receptionist. "I'm so full, so happy."

Back home, she opened her big red-letter edition of the New Testament to Luke 15 and read again about the shepherd who left ninety-nine sheep in the fold, while he went out into the night searching for the one that was lost.

In her small effort, she had shared her Bible lesson with one motorist, one listener in the night. The other ninety-nine, figuratively speaking, had been asleep in their beds in Tinyburg. Suddenly, it was all worthwhile.

Aunt Sarah finished taping all thirteen lessons. She hopes someday a slot will open for a daytime program. If so, and she returns to radio, be sure to listen. You'll hear about apes, donkeys, horses, bears, oxen, crocodiles, camels, deer, goats, lions, hogs, and weasels in the Bible.

And if you're lucky, you'll hear her program on sheep and the Good Shepherd.

The Prettiest Woman
in Tinyburg

Who has the most fun on Valentine's Day in the Tinyburg Church? The children, munching on gaily decorated cupcakes? The teenagers, bringing their dates to a sit-down banquet in the church basement? Or the young married couples, enjoying a potluck?

All of these have loads of fun. But top honors go to the senior adults who invent a new and exciting theme for each year's Valentine party. One of their best parties was February 14, 1987, when prizes went for the best speeches on "Why My Wife's the Prettiest Woman in Tinyburg."

The speech that won first place was by George Mason, a paperhanger. Although he's blind, George has learned to hang any kind of wallpaper, including paper with fancy patterns. Friends wonder how he matches paper so perfectly, entirely by feel, but he keeps them guessing—says it's a "trade secret."

His wife Mae helps in their small decorating business, which they operate out of their home, by estimating the jobs and painting the doors and trim when they paper a room. Before they go on a job, she makes a sketch, in Braille, of each room to be papered.

On the sketches, she pencils in the door and window openings, electrical outlets, and the like. As George runs his fingers over these sketches, he "reads" the shapes of the rooms. This gives him the mental picture necessary to do a neat job.

Here is George's speech about Mae, the one that won first prize:

"Few of you know the details of my blindness, for I don't talk about it unless someone asks. For those who don't know, I lost my sight in World War II—a grenade exploded in my face. Before I was drafted, I was engaged to Tricia, a beautiful, beautiful girl. I was carrying her photo the day I got hurt. We were engaged to be married as soon as the war ended.

"I can still see Tricia, wearing her honey-blonde hair in a pageboy, blue eyes, milky white skin, shy smile, slender, always neatly dressed, soft spoken, a single string of pearls around her neck.

"When I came home, I told Tricia she was free to break our engagement. But she said no, she loved me, and my blindness made no difference. So we set a date, mailed a few invitations to family and friends. It was to be a church wedding—not fancy, but plain and pretty.

"The afternoon of the wedding, I was waiting in a side room with the best man. Time came for the organ prelude. All of a sudden my mouth got so dry I wondered if I could say even the two words 'I do' when the ceremony began.

"After she finished the prelude, I thought the organist would play the Wedding March. Instead, she kept playing the prelude over and over again. Why the delay? I grew more nervous by the minute.

"Then the minister came into the room where I was waiting, put his arms around me, and said, 'George, this is the hardest thing I've ever had to say. But the wedding's been called off.'"

"'Called off!' I shouted, loud enough for guests in the church sanctuary to hear. My first fear was that Tricia was ill, or maybe hurt in an accident driving to the church.

" 'No,' the minister continued. " 'Tricia just called, saying her parents pressured her to change her mind at the last minute. Convinced her she deserves a man for a husband, not an invalid, as she put it.'

"I was already disappointed—but now I grew angry enough to bite her wedding ring in two. I was no invalid! Besides, hadn't I offered her a way out of the engagement? Why did she wait until the last minute to embarrass me in front of everyone?

"I was so hurt I slipped out a side door to the church parking lot. I couldn't bear to face the wedding guests, to listen while they fished around for something to say.

"That night, I made a promise to myself that I'd never love another woman. I'd been burned once—I wouldn't go near the fire again.

"What I failed to understand is that all of life is a risk, that anything we aim for can end in failure. I got so hardened I stopped praying. I said I'd never ask God for anything, as long as I lived. I couldn't risk 'No' for an answer. This was a mistake, too. For if we insulate ourselves against a 'No' from God, we also shut the door to the times God wants to say 'Yes.'

"Soon after, I enrolled in a trade school,

searching for a way a blind fellow could make a living. That's when I met Mae, my wife.

"Mae was an instructor. I told her how I once liked to paint and hang wallpaper, but those days were over. We talked and talked. She helped me see that with retraining, I could be a paperhanger again.

"Best of all, we fell in love. I didn't intend to. I didn't want to. It just happened, slipped up on me. One morning I woke up shouting, 'I'm in love! I'm in love! I'm in love!' In no time, we were married.

"Looking back, I've asked why I broke my vow and married. I've never seen Mae. I have a vague idea what she looks like—the shape of her features. But I can't give you reasons one, two, and three, as to why she's the prettiest girl in Tinyburg.

"What I do know is that I love her because she loved me. And when you've got that kind of marriage, you're a lucky man.

"Is her hair black? Blonde? Red? Grey? Is her skin glowing and radiant, or pale and wrinkled? Are her eyes round and inviting, or sort of crossed and dull? To me, it doesn't matter. What counts is the love she shares with me, which is the best beauty of all. To me, the prettiest woman in Tinyburg is a woman I've never seen. Her name is Mae."

And so ended George's speech. No one was surprised he won first place, and when the judges called the Masons to the front for their award, Mae was delighted to see that it was a framed, full-color reproduction of an essay, "The Garden." Although George couldn't see the beauty of the light-pink parchment and the dark-blue letters, he fell in love with its message when Mae read it to him:

The Garden

WHEN God created a home for the first man and woman to love and live in, He turned His back on marble and stone and oak and cedar. Instead, He formed an Eden of palms and ferns, kissed with dewdrops on daisies and raindrops on roses. And to this day, we taste the sweetest love when we find a door that opens wide upon a lovely garden.

YES, everyone loves a garden, whether a tiny patio where petunias bloom in pots and herbs sprout from window boxes, a farm garden where cabbages mingle with marigolds, or a formal garden on an English hillside, neatly hedged with boxwood and privet.

BUT favorite of favorites is a garden heavy with the perfume of love. The greens and pastels of spring gardens sing of young and waking love. The lush foliage of summer gardens tells of passionate and pregnant love. The subtle browns and golds of autumn gardens speak of proven love, rich in fabric.

And the red berries and shiny evergreens of winter gardens paint a serene and accepting love.

THE choicest garden is a shared garden. And so with love, for there is no love apart from shared love. Selfish is the prison-garden that locks within itself the love that's meant for others. Like the tendrils of a growing plant, love reaches out to touch and bless. Like the aroma of honeysuckle, love permeates the hidden corners of lives beyond its own.

NOW hear the secret of the garden: **It blooms to make others happy, not to make them good.** Likewise with love, for love aims to please the beloved, not to reform. We can no more make someone good than we can make bluebells bloom in a blizzard. What we can do is love them through the gates of happiness. And the wonder is that when folks are happy, they are more likely to be good.

THIS is the secret of the garden...this is the miracle of love.

—RJH

A Tinyburg Treat

When Uncle Billy Cutrell volunteered to help contact inactive members in the Tinyburg Church, he was surprised to get the name of a family that missed fifty-one Sundays last year.

When he knocked on their door, the father, Raymond, surprised him with a warm welcome. "Come in this here house and sit yourself down," he began, opening the door wide and giving Uncle Billy a bear hug. "You're here to ask where we've been hiding out."

"How'd you guess?"

"Read it in the newsletter. Your survey's a great idea for ornery folks. My family, well, we have good reasons."

"Mind if I jot them down?" asked Uncle

Billy, reaching for his pen. "Let's begin with January and sort of summarize your excuses."

"No need to summarize. I've got reasons—not excuses—for all fifty-one Sundays.

"For instance, January 2. Uncle Billy, you can't imagine how this house looks after Christmas. Cards, ribbons, toys everywhere. We always take the Sunday after New Year's to clean up. You'd be surprised at the work in sorting and packing. So I say to the kids, 'Look, have all the fun you want, but once Christmas is over, we pitch in and help Mom,' take a whole day."

"On a Sunday?"

"Of course. It wouldn't be fair to dress up and go off to church, leave that mess to their mother.

"Now, the next two Sundays. Uncle Billy, you remember that January ice storm? Didn't melt for ten days. Streets slick as glass. Weather like that, we don't go nowhere. Don't guess you had church?"

Uncle Billy said yes, services were as usual, although attendance was low, then asked, "Did you miss work those ten days?"

"No, no, no, no, no. I've got a family to support. I can't afford to goof off like some who look for any old excuse to stay home."

"I see," said Uncle Billy, scribbling in his notebook. "What about the next Sunday?"

"Who could forget the flu epidemic? We all had it, but the funny thing is, not at the same time. One got over it, then another came down. I guess it was five Sundays around here that someone was sick. Left me with the worst cough. And when you get with crowds, like in church, it makes you cough worse.

"I could never stand someone hacking away, clearing their throats. I go to hear the Preacher, not cough my head off. That's why—and you'll agree we had good reason—we missed the last three Sundays in January and the first two in February.

"Now the third Sunday in February, let me think. I know—that was the Sunday before Washington's birthday. Uncle Billy, one of the finest things ever happened is those three-day weekends.

"Boy, we like them. Gives our family time to do things together. You add Memorial Day, July 4, and Labor Day, that accounts for five or six Sundays we missed. We bought a new camper and whenever we get three days in a row, we take off."

"That brings us to the last Sunday in February," Uncle Billy said.

"I couldn't forget that Sunday, my in-laws'

golden anniversary. Uncle Billy, you should have been there. Rented a big hall for the reception. I said to my kids, 'Look, let's pitch in to give your Grandma and Grandpa a red-letter day.' We worked our heads off.

"Started decorating about 7:00 that Sunday morning—setting up tables, arranging flowers. Yes, we missed church, but like I told the kids, your old grandparents see only one fiftieth anniversary."

"I can see you're a busy family," Uncle Billy said, turning a page in his notebook. "Now for March."

"Easter came in March last year, and school dismissed for a week. So we took off for ten days in Florida. Packed the van and picked up the kids at school on Friday afternoon, didn't come home until Sunday midnight, ten days later.

"I didn't want to count that trip against my vacation, so I called it sick leave. Remember the flu in January? Lots of days I didn't feel like it, but I dragged myself out of bed and worked anyway. Figured I had the sick leave coming.

"Uncle Billy, you ever been to Disney World and the Magic Kingdom? You can't *believe* it. You see things you'd never see on TV! Plus the space center and all those beaches! I told the wife, I said, 'Hon, this is an education. Our kids won't never forget this.'

"Did we attend services in Florida? Come to think of it, we didn't. You know how it is—looking for a strange church, never know when services begin, maybe go straggling in during the middle of the sermon."

Uncle Billy, growing restless, suggested Raymond skip some Sundays and highlight the best excuses.

Raymond ran his finger down the calendar, stopping when daylight saving time began. "Uncle Billy, changing the clock around confuses me. I never remember whether to get up an hour early or an hour late. One year we went to church the usual time and met folks coming out. That cured me. I said no more. One member looked at me as if I couldn't tell time."

"Let's move on to May," sighed Uncle Billy.

"Would you believe that all last winter, my battery never failed? Then in May—warm weather, mind you—we were in the car ready for church, and it wouldn't start to save your life.

"After dinner, a neighbor drove me to buy a new one. Fooled around with it two or three hours. But it was an emergency, as I had no way to get to work on Monday. You know that Bible verse about the ox in the ditch on the Sabbath? Same principle as a dead battery.

"Now to May—oh, yes, Mother's Day. Big, big event at our house. Much more than a potted plant for Mom. We make a *day* of it. The kids serve Mom breakfast in bed. Then start in on dinner. Won't let her lift a finger. It's nice to honor your Mom at church, but mothers deserve more than honor.

"That brings us to the third Sunday in May. The wife, that morning, woke up with the awfulest sick headache you ever heard tell of. Didn't go away 'til afternoon, so me and the kids fixed lunch again, like the Sunday before.

"Then the fourth Sunday in May, my birthday, is always special. Only this year, the wife surprised me with a houseful of company—started coming about Sunday School time. You see, Uncle Billy, our family is close-knit. We may not be in church every time the door opens, but we look after each other."

By now Uncle Billy felt like closing his notebook.

"Wait," interrupted Raymond. "We've just started on June. You've got Father's Day, and before you know it, vacation's here. Last summer I had three weeks coming, so we went to Alaska—drove every mile in our van. Boy, it's a long way. No, we didn't stop for Sunday school or anything. Not sure they have churches in Alaska—leastwise, we didn't see any."

Feeling as if he'd been to Alaska himself, Uncle Billy listened as Raymond droned on and on . . . homecomings, reunions, state fair, birthday dinners, a funeral or two, summer camp, football games, fishing trips. You name it—Raymond and his family did it.

He did perk up when Raymond described the third Sunday in August: "That's the death anniversary of Elvis Presley, when they put on a gig at Graceland Mansion in Memphis—you know, where he's buried and all that. We reserve our motel a year ahead.

"It's really touching—gets next to you— people crying, buying his tapes, putting flowers on his grave. And hot—do you know how humid it gets in Memphis in August? Nurses in white uniforms in first aid tents—and I mean real nurses with their badges and caps and everything, not just women in white dresses. Some tourists fainted, but they've got ice water and stretchers and ambulances, even oxygen.

"The first summer we went, I told the

wife, Hon, some of these folks are making a religion out of this. I think that's pitiful, for I love my Lord and my little church in Tinyburg too much to get carried away with rock stars."

Knowing there was Labor Day, Halloween, Thanksgiving, and Christmas left, Uncle Billy asked Raymond to jump to November.

"Now you take Thanksgiving. When we got married, it was always a hassle whether to spend Thanksgiving with her folks or mine. So the Sunday before, we eat dinner with my folks. The Sunday after, at hers. No way can we squeeze in church, too."

"I notice here," interrupted Uncle Billy, "that the one time you came was the Sunday before Christmas."

"Oh, and did we enjoy it. One of the nicest pageants you'd ever want to see. No, our kids weren't in it. Rehearsals interfere with their homework. But we enjoyed the other children. My, they were cute, dressed like Wise Men and shepherds. Really touches you.

"And our kids, well, they wanted those treats you pass out. Read about them in that bulletin or newsletter thing you mail out. They wondered if it was like Halloween trick-or-treat. And I said no, there's no trick to it. Those good people treat you with candy just for coming to church.

"When I said that, you couldn't tie them at home with a rope. Problem is, if there's a piece of candy on the place, our kids won't go to bed until they eat it. The only bad memory about their Christmas treat is they ate it before they got home. The youngest was sick all night with a stomachache. 'Course I don't blame the church—it wasn't your fault."

As Uncle Billy stood to leave, he put his hand on Raymond's shoulder: "Friend, you made me think. I don't go near all the places you do. Guess I missed less than three services last year. The reason is, I get a treat *every* Sunday."

"How's that?"

"When I open my eyes on Sunday and feel the quietness of the Lord's Day, and listen for the church bell and the sounds of little children on their way to Sunday School, and realize I'm well and in my right mind, and church friends are waiting to shake hands and ask how I feel, and I join in worshiping the Everlasting Father, the Prince of Peace, I guess every Sunday's a Christmas treat.

"And like your kids, I can't save anything back. I drink it all in. So by the next Sunday, I'm hungry for another treat, whether it's a holiday or an ice storm or whatever."

Raymond coughed uneasily and looked

down at the floor. Then softly, "Uncle Billy, this busy old world needs more people like you."

If you're in Tinyburg (which is exactly seven miles south of Pretense) on a Sunday, visit the church. Tell Uncle Billy I sent you, and that you came for a treat. I guarantee you'll find one.

A Cornbread Thanksgiving

Joe and Rose Lawson and their five kids are what you might call an effervescent family. Bubbly, hyperactive, always on the go. Both Joe and Rose come from large families, which means one birthday dinner, family reunion, and wedding anniversary after another. Uncle Billy Cutrell often calls them to ask why they manage to miss so many Sundays from Bible study and preaching.

Although not much of a churchgoer, Joe is civic-minded and people-oriented. Each year, he's a big wheel in the community Thanksgiving dinner for the poor and elderly. He not only helps to publicize the dinner and arrange transportation but also makes yellow cornbread. It's become a tradition. He makes it in big, flat baking pans—acres of it! Golden brown, moist, steaming hot.

You may not think of homemade cornbread on the traditional Thanksgiving menu. But the older people like it and look forward to the big, thick squares, topped with fresh butter.

Early last October the dinner committee contacted Joe, asking if he would again coordinate the transportation and bake the cornbread. The telephone call caught him at a bad time. Fact is, he hadn't felt good all that summer. Why, he didn't know. His appetite was good, his health normal. But there was a nagging depression, a burned-out feeling.

So he replied, rather abruptly, "Get someone else this year. I've done my part. Holidays don't mean what they once did. Halloween isn't over and we're talking Thanksgiving. Stores already pushing Christmas merchandise, and we haven't had one good, killing frost. Gimme, gimme, gimme, that's what it boils down to. No, don't count on me this year."

Rose, overhearing the conversation, was puzzled: "Joseph, this isn't like you. The dinner's fun! And seeing all the old people, and how they eat every crumb of your homemade bread."

"Ask someone else to bake the cornbread," he snapped. "Use a mix. Anyone can do it."

"Care if me and the kids help?"

"Suit yourself. But don't pester me anymore. I may skip Thanksgiving altogether. Christmas as well, who knows? Too much folderol."

Nine-year-old Dawn asked, "Mother, we *will* go and help serve the grandmas and grandpas, won't we?"

"We'll see. Your Daddy's upset about something, but maybe he'll get over it."

"No, I'm not upset," Joe thundered. "But I am burnt out, making other people happy who have nothing to be happy about. Feed them one day, forget them the next. Half of them never bother to say 'Thank you.' Just another day, another meal."

Rose, tempted to argue that the community dinner was more than just another meal, bit her tongue and gathered up a load of clothes for the washer.

Joe did promise to take the family to church one Sunday before the holidays. "But not every Sunday," he warned. "Just one, and get it over with before time to take up those Christmas offerings."

They agreed on the second Sunday in November. "You can take the kids to the programs nearer Christmas," he told Rose, "but this is all for me."

The members greeted Joe warmly, no one questioning why he hadn't attended services since Mother's Day in May.

The Preacher spoke on Christmas joy: "All normal people want to be happy. And I believe God wants us to be happy. But it's hard to be happy when bad things happen: illness, hard luck, the death of loved ones, a home that burns at Christmas, a bad wreck on the highway." He added that some people are unhappy by choice. He quoted Abraham Lincoln. "Most folks are about as happy as they make up their minds to be." He then defined two kinds of happiness:

"Happiness by *chance* means we feel good if everything's going our way. Happiness by *choice* means we look for something to be glad about, even when our dreams turn sour."

Then he told the following story to illustrate what he meant. The story was so realistic that some of the children thought it actually happened:

"Once upon a time a wealthy businessman died and left a bequest to pay for a Thanksgiving feast every November. There was only one requirement: guests at the dinner had to be the unhappiest people in town.

Not necessarily the oldest, poorest, or sickest. Just the unhappiest.

"Whoever wanted a free ticket was required to write a short letter, telling why they were unhappy. After reading the letters, the judges concluded that many of the miserable people fitted into four categories:

"First, the suspicious—persons who see hidden motives in everything others say or do. They never take anyone at face value. As a result, they distrust everyone. They have no close friends. Naturally, they're sad during the holidays.

"In the second category are the cynics. They focus their cynicism on the entire world, including the power and goodness of God. Just as those who are suspicious see no good in people, so the cynics see no good in society as a whole. Psalm 1:1 says they 'sit in the seat of the scornful.'"

The congregation listened as the Preacher described the third and fourth kinds of unhappy people:

"Group three has a martyr complex. They behave like sacrificial lambs. They delight in self-pity. They see themselves as a kind of floor mat where others wipe their muddy shoes.

"I call the fourth group hedonists. The opposite of martyrs who live only for others, hedonists live only for themselves. To them, pleasure is happiness. This means material comforts, luxuriant automobiles, fine homes, big salaries, prime rib every night.

"Yes, these were the kinds of people who, in the story, qualified for the free dinner. When time came for the Thanksgiving dinner, some guests drove up in limousines, while others walked. Some were as healthy as Olympic athletes, while others hobbled in on crutches. Some wore the latest fashions, while others dressed in rags. They were so different, yet alike in one respect: each guest had convinced the screening committee that he or she was miserable.

"You wouldn't have wanted to be there yourself, because the guests, wringing their hands in despair, spent the whole time whining and complaining."

Thus ended the Preacher's story about the Thanksgiving feast for unhappy people.

Dawn, one of Joe's five kids, listened with awe. Her eyes widened as she visualized the Tinyburg Community Center filled with griping guests. She shuddered to think about it. But childlike, she imagined how she could put up with their complaints if her Daddy would help again this year, and they could all go as a family.

That afternoon, Dawn interrupted Joe while he was reading the Sunday sports page:

"Daddy...."

"Yes?"

"Daddy, could we eat at the free Thanksgiving dinner, even if we don't help this year?"

"Of course not," he snapped. "What gave you such a silly idea? The dinner's for the poor and elderly. It's not for folks like us, because we can afford our own turkey and goodies."

"But, Daddy, we qualify for the dinner."

"Stop arguing, Dawn. We're neither poor nor old. Whatever gave you the idea we're invited?"

Dawn replied, in all innocence, "But you've been sad a long time, and the Preacher said the dinner's for sad people, not the poor."

"So what?"

"That means even if we're not poor, we can go because we're sad."

"Dawn, do you think that story was true? The Preacher made it up to illustrate his sermon. That was a make-believe dinner. His story doesn't apply to the community dinner here in Tinyburg."

"Then why did he tell the story?"

"As I said once, he told it to, uh, to...."

Then, "Oh, forget it," as he slammed the paper down and stalked out of the room.

Joe said little the rest of the day. I guess he was thinking about cornbread and old people, cornbread and lonely people, cornbread and happy people, cornbread and sad people. "Wish cornbread had never been invented," he whispered to himself.

The next morning when he raised the bedroom shade, Joe looked out over distant farmland at a field of corn stalks, standing stark and dry and brown in the cold morning. The sun's rays fell on the patch of corn, turning it to a golden brown. For a moment, it reminded him of a giant pan of yellow cornbread!

After breakfast, he called Clay Barker, food chairman for the community dinner: "Ordered all the food?"

"No, just the turkeys. Getting ready to buy the rest today."

"Then remember to pick up twenty pounds of yellow cornmeal. And make sure it's yellow. One year you bought white cornmeal, and folks complained."

"Wasn't my fault," Clay apologized. "They switched on me at the wholesale house."

"Well, no switching this time, or I'll make you take it back," joked Joe.

Each year at the dinner in the Tinyburg Community Center, the crowd seems to get bigger and the food tastes better, especially Joe's yellow cornbread. This year was no exception. And the entire Lawson family pitched in to help—Joe, Rose, and all five kids. Every church in town provided a van, bus, or car to pick up guests, especially the elderly. Over half of the residents from the Tinyburg Nursing Home came. For those who couldn't, the ladies fixed food trays which Joe delivered in person.

An elderly patient, her mind almost gone, bit into a thick chunk of Joe's cornbread and dreamed she was a housewife again, baking bread for her growing family.

Another patient, who ordinarily has little appetite, bit into his square of cornbread topped with home-churned butter, and dreamed he was on the farm again, and it was dinner time, and cold and blustery outdoors, but his wife had baked a big pan of cornbread, and the aroma of the melting butter filled the entire farmhouse, and all was well, and he was very, very happy.

Helen's Bible

"Is this the pastor of the Tinyburg Church?"

"Yes. May I help you?"

"You don't know me, but I'm calling long distance about my great aunt, Helen Norman, who passed away last night."

"Norman? I don't recognize the name. Where did she live?"

"Aunt Helen lived in a nursing home here in Ohio," said the caller, identifying himself as Claude. "Years ago, she taught third grade in Tinyburg. I doubt if anyone remembers, for that was sixty years ago, and she was ninety-three when she died. Anyway, she loved the people there. Always said she wanted to be buried in Tinyburg.

"Fact is, for several years, she's sent a

couple of dollars to your postmaster, asking him to mail her a Christmas card postmarked Tinyburg. Purely for sentiment—but meant everything to her."

The Preacher said of course he would take care of the service, adding, "I like to include something personal about the deceased in my funeral messages. Since I didn't know Helen, could you describe her, give some biographical details?"

"Reverend, I'm embarrassed to say so, but I don't have that information where I can lay my hands on it. You see, she outlived all her children, and I didn't know her all that well. This sounds awful, but I can't even tell you where she was born."

"Don't apologize," the Preacher reassured Claude. "Families move about these days, get scattered and uprooted. I'm glad your aunt thought enough of Tinyburg to be brought back here. Maybe you could look through her personal effects, for older persons often write down suggestions for their funerals."

"That reminds me," Claude answered. "Aunt Helen loved her Bible. Read it daily and also used it for clippings, old letters, bits of poetry. It's a treasure of memorabilia."

"Sounds like we're onto something," replied the Preacher. "If it's okay with you, I'd like to leaf through her Bible. But I'll need it a day ahead of the funeral."

"I'll send it by overnight express mail," Claude offered. "You should have it tomorrow."

When the Preacher unwrapped Helen Norman's Bible, it was like opening a family scrapbook. Not only had she written notes in the margins and underlined favorite verses, but inside were old snapshots, letters, wedding invitations, and birthday cards, plus pages of poetry she'd clipped from magazines.

It was like tracing Helen Norman's spiritual pilgrimage to read the verses she highlighted. This gave the Preacher an idea: "Instead of reading from my pulpit Bible at the funeral, I'll use Helen's."

The next day the Preacher led a beautiful service for the handful of kinfolk who accompanied Helen's body from Ohio, but he did so with the same dignity as if the funeral chapel were full.

"It's evident that Helen loved her family," he began, "for her Bible bulged with photos and clippings about them. She also collected poems, and in her memory I want to read a few of her favorites. In closing, I'll comment on her favorite Bible verse.

"The first is 'Little Boy Blue' by Eugene

Field. Her comment reads, 'This poem was a favorite of my third grade pupils in Tinyburg. I often read it to them. His make-believe soldiers and other toys just fascinated them.'

The little toy dog is covered with dust,
    But sturdy and staunch he stands;
And the little toy soldier is red with rust,
    And his musket moulds in his hands.
Time was when the little toy dog was new,
    And the soldier was passing fair,
And that was the time when our Little Boy
    Blue Kissed them and put them there.

"Now don't you go till I come," he said,
    "And don't you make any noise!"
So toddling off to his trundle-bed
    He dreamt of the pretty toys.
And as he was dreaming, an angel song
    Awakened our Little Boy Blue,—
Oh, the years are many, the years are long,
    But the little toy friends are true!

Ay, faithful to Little Boy Blue they stand,
    Each in the same old place,
Awaiting the touch of a little hand,
    The smile of the little face.
And they wonder, as waiting those long
      years through,
    In the dust of that little chair,
What has become of our Little Boy Blue
    Since he kissed them and put them
      there.

As the Preacher read the poem in the hushed chapel, it sounded old and quaint, as if from another era. But Helen's family listened in awe, as if they were her pupils, eight years old again, and she their teacher, in a faraway classroom now smothered with dust.

Next he chose a verse by Emily Dickinson. In the margin, Helen had written, "Oh, how these lines touched me when I first read them, reminding me that death comes for everyone, whether prepared or not."

> Because I could not stop for Death,
> He kindly stopped for me;
> The carriage held but just ourselves
> And immortality.

"This next poem is by James Whitcomb Riley, the Hoosier poet of Indiana. I selected it because it meant so much to Helen. In the margin she wrote that when she taught here in Tinyburg, one little pupil was always talking about her Aunt Mary on a nearby farm. Riley's Aunt Mary was a different person, of course, but his colorful verses capture the nostalgia of a bygone day which are the same:

> Wasn't it pleasant, O brother mine,
> In those old days of the lost sunshine
>   Of youth—when the Saturday's chores
>   were through,

And the "Sunday wood" in the kitchen,
  too,
And we went visiting, "me and you,"
    Out to Old Aunt Mary's!

We cross the pasture, and through the
    wood
Where the old gray snag of the poplar
    stood,
  Where the hammering red-heads
    hopped awry,
  And the buzzard "raised" in the clearing
    sky,
  And lolled and circled, as we went by,
    Out to Old Aunt Mary's.

Why, I see her now in the open door,
Where the little gourds grew up the sides,
    and o'er
  The clapboard roof!—And her face—ah,
    me!
  Wasn't it good for a boy to see—
  And wasn't it good for a boy to be
    Out to Old Aunt Mary's?

The jelly—the jam and the marmalade,
And the cherry and quince "preserves" she
    made!
  And the sweet-sour pickles of peach and
    pear,
  With cinnamon in 'em, and all things
    rare!—
  And the more we ate was the more to
    spare,
    Out to Old Aunt Mary's!

And the old spring-house in the cool green
    gloom

Of the willow-trees, and the cooler room
  Where the swinging-shelves and the
    crocks were kept—
  Where the cream in a golden languor
    slept
  While the waters gurgled and laughed
    and wept
    Out to Old Aunt Mary's!

And O, my brother, so far away,
This is to tell you she waits *today*
  To welcome us:—Aunt Mary fell
  Asleep this morning, whispering, "Tell
  The boys to come!" And all is well
    Out to Old Aunt Mary's!

The Preacher concluded Helen's eulogy by reading 2 Timothy 1:12: "I am not ashamed: for I know whom I have believed, and am persuaded that he is able to keep that which I have committed unto him against that day."

"This is the most heavily underscored verse in Helen's Bible. It had to be close to her heart.

"The sentimental poems she treasured about Little Boy Blue and Old Aunt Mary speak of this life, which soon fades away. The Bible verse speaks of the life to come, the one that lasts for eternity. It's fitting, when we conduct the last rites for our loved ones, to recall what gave them pleasure here on earth. It's also fitting to speak of their faith in the next life, as evidenced by 2 Timothy 1:12.

"Helen surely treasured this Bible verse because it speaks with finality: 'I *know* whom I have believed.' Helen wasn't guessing about eternal life.

"Is one boasting when he claims to *know* his salvation is sure? I'll answer by saying that the verse Helen underlined *is* boastful. But it's bragging on *God,* not Helen. *He* is the able one!"

At the cemetery, Claude thanked the Preacher on behalf of the family: "We appreciate the personal touch, the way you made the memories live again. Truly, she has come home to Tinyburg. You made us feel good. Thank you."

The Preacher replied that he'd better return Grandma's Bible, so the family could take it back to Ohio. Then he added, "Be sure to keep this little clipping by Robert Louis Stevenson. There wasn't time to read it at the funeral. It tells us why Helen wanted Tinyburg for her resting place:

> Under the wide and starry sky,
> Dig the grave and let me lie.
> Glad did I live and gladly die,
>   And I laid me down with a will.

This be the verse you grave for me:
Here he lies where he longed to be;
Home is the sailor, home from sea,
  And the hunter home from the hill.